MHQ1272992

DAKGHAR:

THE HOUSE THAT CALLS

A Novel in Four Voices

ASHIS GUPTA

BAYEUX ARTS
DIGITAL · TRADITIONAL PUBLISHING

Dakghar: The House That Calls

Publication: December 2019
Printed in Canada
Published in Canada by
Bayeux Arts Digital - Traditional Publishing
2403, 510 6th Avenue, S.E.
Calgary, Canada T2G 1L7

www.bayeux.com

Cover design by Alexiev Gandman
Book design by Lumina

Library and Archives Canada Cataloguing in Publication

Title: Dakghar: the house that calls: a novel in four voices / Ashis Gupta
Names: Gupta, Ashis, 1940- author.
Identifiers: Canadiana (print) 20190157720 | Canadiana (ebook)
20190157739 | ISBN 9781988440354 (hardcover) |
ISBN 9781988440361 (HTML)
Classification: LCC PS8613.U68 D34 2019 | DDC C813/.6—dc23

The ongoing publishing activities of Bayeux Arts Digital - Traditional Publishing
under its varied imprints are supported by the Government of Alberta, Alberta
Multimedia Development Fund, and the Government of Canada through the Book
Publishing Industry Development Program.

Dedicated to victims of tyranny, oppression,
and racism

Warsaw, Poland, is as much a city of beauty as it is one of memories, not unlike many other great cities of the world. But there is a difference – the Warsaw Ghetto, ravaged and made desolate by the Nazis in April 1943. The spirits of more than 50,000 murdered Jews still haunt parts of Warsaw, so it is said.

On July 15, 1942, the Jewish population already under siege in Warsaw, residents of an orphanage on Sliska Street, run by Dr. Janusz Korczak, staged the play, "The Post Office," **(Bengali - <u>Daak Ghawr</u>)** *by the poet Rabindranath Tagore. It was as much an act of defiance as an assertion of the indomitable human spirit.*

October 11, 1998

"Tetsuo is the midwife to our dreams," said Martin Fisher. "But for him, we would all have faced terrible ends."

What my father meant was that Tetsuo, who had a sleek office on the topmost floor of a Warsaw glass tower, was something of a god. The slightest touch of his hand unlocked vast stores of wealth and power beyond our imagination. Tetsuo touched our lives. Tetsuo gave us voices. Tetsuo shared our songs. Tetsuo set us free.

The first voice was spread out to dry on a chain of diamonds. People gathered around, in hushed silence, waiting for it to speak. The chain swayed in the wind, or so it seemed, sending flashes of lightning that jolted the crowd to shivers of ecstasy. Their polite murmurs and the sigh of the wind were all the sounds I could hear, for the voice remained silent. It remained locked in my memory.

Ever so slowly, time passed. One by one, the crowd began to drift away until only a single curious dog, a brown mongrel, remained behind, playfully pawing an empty pop can rattling near the sewer, sniffing at the crumpled sandwich wrappings fluttering in the gutter. Suddenly, the voice came to life with a soft whistling noise. The startled dog leapt up and ran to catch up with its departing owner. The whistling grew louder, punctuated by the staccato gurgling of boiling water. The flashes of light shooting from the diamonds mingled with the hissing steam and appeared more like hooded snakes blinded by mist frantically striking in every direction. The gaunt old man in a faded green suit had so far remained motionless and unnoticed on the steps to the jewelry store. Now he started to cough, his body shaking violently, his vacant eyes staring into space. That's where I found him.

The brown dog didn't run very far. The crowd had reassembled only half a block away. I dragged the bewildered old man there. He knew me, he loved me, and came uncomplainingly with me.

The crowd stood in silence, unable or unwilling to move any closer to the woman. Shadows from a balcony up above lay stencilled on the sidewalk and on her body, relentlessly pinning her to the ground, two parallel lines like the dark oars I often saw resting against a rotting boathouse wall along the Vistula. Some had children with them, children they held tightly pressed to their bodies. Others stared uncomprehendingly. A young girl knelt on the sidewalk and sobbed into her hands. Hers was the only sound there until a delivery truck came round and screeched to a halt under an ornamental street lamp strangely out of place among the modern store fronts. Surprised and curious, the driver leapt out of the cab, slammed the door shut, and walked up to the crowd. Marek and I edged closer to the woman.

The delivery man, now standing over us, was about to ask a question when he was silenced by others who raised their fingers to their lips. The woman was trying to say something to Marek who was now bent over her, holding her head in his hands. She raised her fingers gently to the old man's paltry tufts of grey hair. I wanted to touch her too, but I couldn't. I couldn't move. I felt rooted to the stone slabs under my feet.

"Don't cry, Marek," said the woman. Her voice was weak, her glassy eyes hardly open. "Don't cry," she repeated even more softly, barely forming the words with her lips.

"How can I not cry?" said the old man, his voice startlingly loud in contrast to hers. "You were more than half my life, and now you're leaving me."

The brown dog ran through the crowd and stopped abruptly next to Marek, wagging its tail, still curious. Its presence upset some in the crowd who, annoyed, turned their heads looking for its owner. A middle-aged woman wearing dark glasses quickly left the crowd and coaxed the dog back by his collar, all the while looking apologetically at the faces surrounding her. The truck sped away, the driver calling someone on his cell-phone, smiling to himself.

Another man quietly left the crowd and walked over to a bunch of flowers fallen near the woman. He picked up the flowers, then looked about uncertainly not knowing what to do with them. The flowers were already starting to wilt in the strong sun. The man stared for a while at the flowers in his hand, then placed them carefully against the display window of a computer store and muttered something, perhaps a prayer, perhaps a swear. Nothing seemed to be open on this street this Sunday, except the flower and vegetable stands the woman was returning from some distance away. Without them, Sundays in Warsaw would be so gloomy.

If the woman uttered another word, I never heard it. By the time the ambulance and the police arrived, she was dead. I held the old man's hand and helped him stand. A police officer walked over to us and asked if we knew the old woman. The old man simply nodded his head as if to say no; as if to say, yes. Who knows? I remained silent. Someone interrupted the officer to say she was present at the scene before the old man and I had come along. This was only half the truth, but the officer shifted his attention to this woman and let us walk free. We heard the ambulance drive off just as we were entering the apartment. The moment the sound died away, the music started in my head.

ONE

For years I have tried in vain to shut it out of my mind. It was exactly fifty years later that I suddenly remembered. How in the summer of 1940 we were startled to find that all of us were apparently living in a plague-infested part of Warsaw. We were surprised, to say the least, for there had been no unusual deaths. Fifty years later, I look at myself in the mirror and can't notice any difference from fifty years and a day ago. Yes, there are some dark shadows under the eyes, but I have always had them. Never get to sleep at nights. It seems I have hardly slept in fifty years. Of course, my hair is almost gone, but that too didn't happen in a single night. Or did it?

I proceeded to examine the skin on my face and discovered I really needed my glasses for that. The glasses have grown thicker over the years, but what's so unusual about that? Still, the face does look like the face of an old man, with a sad, untended beard. I am not too thrilled about looking closely at my body. The flesh hangs a little under the arms, the chest is somewhat sunk. Nothing gross, but it does look wasted. And the little runt hanging between the legs has all but gone to sleep. Could all these signs be symptoms of the plague, I thought, as I had thought fifty years ago. Perhaps they were. Maybe it's just that medical science didn't know enough about them.

Then something happened that filled my heart with dread. It was the others who suddenly appeared next to me in the mirror. They were behind me, they were on all sides of me. Some even lay suspended in air, or hanging danger- ously from the upper edges of the mirror. Some had faces of cats and lobsters. Others had wheels screwed to their hands. They were awful. Strangely, they looked much like me in their nakedness, but that was not why I seemed to recognize each one of them. They were all faces I had seen somewhere. Could it have been in passing? No, I felt as if I had looked into their eyes, maybe even held them in my arms. Strange as it may seem, I could clearly see myself in the mirror as I was fifty years ago. Is it possible that I have survived with the plague for fifty years?

Of course, all this is a lie. You must realize that I cannot see. I am seventy years old, blind, and an inveterate liar. But you must forgive me, for my world was suddenly abbrevi- ated fifty years ago. Totally unexpected, for we were young and it was a time when the world was supposed to bloom in front of our eyes. It is easy to fill a cramped, shrunken world with lies.

Who knows whether for such
a time as this thou hast been
brought to the kingdom.
                                        - Esther iv.14

* * *

Voice One: Matthew

One-One

I had to open the windows, I thought, putting down a bunch of yellowing sheets of paper that were part of what was supposed to have been Marek's diary. As I continued to rummage through his papers I began to sense how similar we were in many ways. But I didn't need to imagine myself looking into a mirror to discover others crowding around my face. I have lived each day for the past six years with another me by my side. His face, his body, his eyes. they are the same as mine. And yet, we couldn't be more different from one other. He hates strong smells, and that is why I had to open the windows just then. At least, I can be considerate. I suppose all old people have a funny smell, not good or bad, but funny. It must linger awhile after they are gone. I found it gathering around Martin as he grew older. My father must have been about sixty or so - with already a whiff of this - when I first met Marek. Until then, I don't think I really knew anyone old except for Martin Fisher, my father. He really didn't look that old, except that sometimes he tried to do things which made him look silly and old. Like trying to do cartwheels on the beach in the summer to impress someone or the other visiting the sea coast like us. I felt quite embarrassed. Marek gave off the same kind of smell, only much stronger. Now Marek is gone.

There was an added touch of mothballs or dry cleaning detergent or whatever it is that gives old clothes their distinctive smell. When I pointed this out to him one day, Marek said, "How remarkable!" He said he knew of a place where he had sniffed the same smell in bundles of clothes stacked one on top of the other. And then, suddenly, he couldn't smell it any more, even though the bundles kept piling up. Oh! he said there was a smell all right, but it wasn't from the clothes even though they often bundled up burnt flesh and dried blood with the clothes. Which seemed a silly thing to do because it was easier to wash one piece of clothing than an entire bundle. But, no, this other smell was definitely not from the clothes. Marek must have been as sensitive to smell as one of me. Until he lost the power, or simply gave up.

Like Marek, I too must be lying if I keep insisting there are two of me. But it is true. One of us went to prison for a crime in which he had no part, absolutely none. But how can you prove one of you is innocent, while the other one of you might be slightly guilty? Marek never faced the problem. For him and the thousand and more images like him that he claims he saw all the time there was no question of guilt or innocence. They were victims of the plague, one and all. I wonder if plagues make any distinction between one victim and the other, between the innocent and the guilty.

The other one of me loves fragrances. Maybe not old folks' smells, but sweet smells that make you feel the wind is rushing through your hair, that electrify your body with desire. I am glad some of the electricity had faded before I went to prison, or I might have ended my life during the first few terrible weeks. This was the guilty I, touched with doubt and shame, forever seeking refuge behind passing clouds of love.

To be starved of love without being starved of the desire for love is something I could never bear. That would be reason enough for me to end my life. Tetsuo mocked me for having said that. He thought music was sufficient reason to wish for eternal life, and he after all was the keeper of music, a sacred trust.

There was little love to be had, it seems, for the other I. I desperately sought my father's love. To find it, I plunged myself into books, hoping to endear myself to him through them. Martin Fisher was a lover of books, and a storehouse of wondrous tales. As a young boy, I would walk with him to the cliffs overlooking our town, really a village hugging the highway, where very little happened except in winter when snow sometimes closed the roads and the truckers wandered in looking for women and shelter. In a way, I was glad Matthew and Misha had found each other. Now we could each go our own way. Which meant I could be happy and sad at the same time, revolted and attracted simultaneously, love and hate the same person without appearing silly to myself or to others.

Matthew and Misha, we've been through a lot these last few years. And the last few days, there has been too much sadness, too many shocks. I feel like I'm just coming out of a fever. The head's a little light and woozy, my steps faltering and unsteady, cold flashes come and go, covering my face and neck with perspiration. Suddenly, it seems I am faced with other things to deal with than the details of Marek's funeral and whatever might come later. Thank God it's over. I wonder if we buried him eventually in one of the holes in the cemetery he claimed he hung around in while dodging the Germans after he escaped from Treblinka to Warsaw. Now I have to worry about things like the post-mortem reports which are of some interest to me, I suppose, even though my skin condition appears to have just about cleared up. Why I am to be burdened with these reports and other matters is not very clear to me. Perhaps it is because Marek has left all his possessions to me. That's what Mr. Nowakowski, my father's lawyer friend, called to tell me last week. Strange how all this makes me feel much older than I felt yesterday. Death ripens us all, doesn't it? Those who die and those who are left behind.

Marek would say that the only way to survive death is to think of it as a joyous celebration. So I didn't feel shocked or surprised when the buzzer rang sometime later and Connie walked in with some baguettes, cheese and a bottle of champagne. Connie and I had talked about it, so it didn't seem wholly inappropriate. Tetsuo, the record company executive and Connie's former lover, tended to think of death - despite his overwhelming optimism - in more solemn terms. To him, death was like casting off your daytime clothes and putting on a tuxedo to travel from the natural world to the supernatural. Tetsuo wasn't very clear on what went on in the supernatural world. "Nothing," he was fond of saying, somewhat enigmatically. "Music perhaps?" I asked. "Maybe," he answered with a shrug. Lydia was more positive. "We will meet in another world," she would tell me. "What's the good of finding love if you can't keep it? Forever." She seemed innocently confident of eternity.

I realized these weighty philosophical matters were best set aside the moment Connie entered the apartment. "I'm glad you've opened the windows," she said, taking off her jacket and sitting down to take off her shoes. I stood watching her slender legs, burnt no doubt to a light almond on some sun-drenched beach, as she carefully pulled off her stockings. Then she stood up and shook her dark Arabian Nights hair from side to side. This proved too much for me, especially in my weakened condition. I walked over to her, folded her in my arms, and fastened my lips on her mouth while our tongues twisted and turned like eels squirming in a bucket. I found myself gasping for breath when our lips parted. "Don't we have work to do?" she asked, as she let her dress flutter to the ground.

"We do," I nodded, as I lifted the weight of her breasts in my hands. I kissed each breast separately, taking my time, allowing my tongue to brush the nipples like a feather. Then I squeezed the breasts together and buried my face in them. This was the stuff of my prison dreams I dreamt night and day. They filled the cracks of my daily routine, plastered over the monotony which is a prison's greatest curse.

I thought I heard her voice coming from somewhere far away. "I am not ready yet," she was saying. "Why don't we first finish what we have to do?"

Little by little, I eased myself down from the clouds. Yes, there were seemingly important things to attend to. Marek's stuff had to be placed in boxes and put in storage. The apartment needed to be cleaned. Really clean, the lawyer warned me, or there'd be cleaning charges. Suddenly I began to feel very tired. "I've already started on his papers," I told Connie. " See, the empty boxes are spilling out of the closet. Why don't you tackle the books?"

"I've always had my eyes on his books," said Connie. "All the strangest Eastern mystics and poets, not to mention more familiar names like Goethe, Dostoevsky, and Heine. Oh yes, and the historian, Heinrich Graetz." She took a quick peek outside the windows and came to me and gave me a hug. "Do you know any of them?" she asked.

"Yes, I do," I told her, which was the truth since I had come across most of the great writers in prison.

"You don't mind me working naked, do you?" she asked suddenly.

"I love it," I replied, and I meant it. "It'll get warmer. I'm taking off my shirt too."

There were two bookshelves side by side to the left of a large window directly behind the worn but perfectly functional sofa for which Olga had bought, in happier days, a bright throw-cover with a mock brocade coat-of-arms in yellow and black. I tried to remember the store where she had bought it, but couldn't.

Connie lifted a handful of books from one of the shelves and piled them on the coffee table. Then she fetched a cardboard box from the closet, one of the many I had carried to the apartment from the nearby supermarket where I used to shop for Marek. The check-out girls all loved me. They remembered me.

"There's a lot of dust on them books," I warned her from my chair in front of the writing table where Marek kept all his letters, all his work. I couldn't see her from where I sat, which was just as well.

"You're right," she answered. "I think I'll move over to the other table."

I was reading odd pages of Marek's writing so I didn't pay too much attention to Connie. There was a narrow table directly in front of the window behind the sofa. When I happened to look back a short while later, I was horrified to see Connie sitting naked on the table going through a fresh pile

of books one by one. I'll never know from where this puritan-
ical streak got into me. It bothers me. Actually, Connie was
a pretty sight. It's just that there were already enough peep
show stalls on the street not far away, and I didn't want to add
Marek's living room window to the list of local options.

"What're you doing?" I cried as I ran and pulled her away
from the window which, while it didn't face any apartments,
was perfectly visible from a park across the road.

"You're such a prude," said Connie, laughing.

I thought for a moment and replied, "Well, a part of me is
something of a prude. But another part would feel perfectly at
ease making love on the table by the window."

"I see," said Connie as she flopped down on the sofa, still
holding on to a book she was reading earlier.

"I hope you're filling up some of those boxes, not just reading," I said, retreating to the sofa. I lit a cigarette and lay back,
savouring my first complete day of freedom after four years in
prison.

One-Two

Martin Fisher had worked behind the scenes and made it possible for me to come out after Marek's death. I realize now how little I know of my father. Never told me much about himself. "It's not right for young people to go abroad before they mature," he said, commenting on what he saw as a change for the worse in me. He thought it was entirely due to my leaving our secure roots in the British Columbia mountains for the greater uncertainties of Europe. But I knew the real reason. Lydia, Lydia, Lydia. The flower lady, my sometimes mother. She's the reason why I find myself torn between Matthew and Misha. As Matthew, I keep trying to understand my mother's inability to be a mother, to be anything for that matter. I also try to mean something to Martin, something other than a responsibility as he calls it. It's easy for others to see that not much love is lost between my father and me. I feel sorry for him in a way. Not that he needs my sympathy. He doesn't need anybody's. He's tough.

Of the two favours I have to thank Martin Fisher for, Lydia is number one. And that is where Misha comes in, this terrible fear in me that the love between Misha and Lydia, which happened so suddenly, kept blossoming over time, might just as suddenly disappear some day. Misha tries to make Matthew understand what he feels, but each seems to live in a world of his own.

How to please my father has been my biggest concern. Should I spend more time in sports, which was somewhat difficult inside prison? Should I try to excel in the sciences, for I felt that would surely impress Martin as nothing else would. Now, there were times when this struck me as something of a paradox, for I was to discover that my father secretly harboured literary ambitions even as he prided himself as a man of intellectual intensity and raw physical action. I remember him bounding across boulders and streams as he often led me to a spot where he believed all life began. I have yet to see any place more beautiful than Burgess Pass, so close to our home that I often thought of it as a private retreat. On weekends, Martin would cook his usual buckwheat pancakes and bacon and then we would hop into our Ford pickup for the half hour ride to Takakkaw Falls. Once there, we'd walk, skirting past the Whiskey Jack Hostel and climbing up to the Burgess Ridge. By the time we reached the high spot in the late afternoon, the falling sun would almost always gild the snow-covered President Range in gold while, below us, Emerald Lake glowed darkly like a brooding, priceless jewel with fathomless histories of passion and intrigue sealed in its heart. With a view so rich, so unforgettable, it was easy to believe why God might have chosen Burgess Shale to begin life on earth.

Martin Fisher became something of a hero in our little town - a village, really, as I keep reminding myself - after he came back from a war in the desert where he claimed he had fought and defeated an enemy far more powerful than the Saddam Hussein whose butt he was awful glad to have had a chance to kick. The other enemy was Fire. Something makes me think he has been fighting fires all his life. But when he sometimes introduced himself to strangers and they asked him what he did, at first I would be surprised to hear him say, "I'm in the oil business." I would've thought the correct answer would have been to say that he was in the fire business. I understand now that to have said he was in the fire business might have implied that he was a fireman or perhaps even a fire insurance salesman. But he was neither of these, and it was an oil company that paid his wages, and paid him handsomely.

Martin was part of a crack team of engineers put together by a greater hero than my father, a certain Red Adair, and together they battled the raging oil fires in the desert war for weeks and months. Father was always modest about his exploits and showered praise on the team as a whole. He was all for team-work. Without the help of his buddies, he thought he would never have survived his first week on assignment somewhere near a city called Al-Basra. Actually, there was an accident and he lost two of his mates on the fifth morning. I wonder if he still thrashes around and screams in his sleep that Jerry and Butch were like two tiny tongues of fire careening helplessly through the burning fields and zeroing in on him. He saw them rolling, twisting madly on the bed of fire. Saw them melt like wax and sink into the ooze of the fields of fire.

On those nights when he woke me up, I would quietly go up to his bed, grab his hand, and that would be enough to snap him out of his nightmare. It was in moments like these that I truly missed my mother who had gone mad and had to be shut up in a nut-house in Ponoka, not far from where we lived. I would lie awake in bed after these terrible dreams and wish my father had a girl-friend or someone like that who might sleep with him and shake him out of his nightmares before he got too far into them. When I saw the IMAX film on the oil fires during a weekend visit to Calgary, I could easily imagine Jerry and Butch, their bodies on fire, madly screaming out of one ball of fire only to be swallowed by another, roaring towards them from east or west or south or who knows from where. The theatre itself was like a wheel of fire with me in the middle. I was luckier than Butch and Jerry. Of course, there was no escape for them. They must have melted, just as my father saw them, then evaporated or become transformed into two grains of sand, or even settled down in the pool of oil below the sand. Hard to tell. There were moments I felt quite scared in the movie hall. It seemed something of a scientific miracle to me that we could sit in that wheel of fire and come out of it alive, until I reminded myself that we were only watching a movie. Afterwards, I kept muttering the name 'Adair, Adair' over and over again. The name had a marvellous ring to it as it tripped over the tongue and ended in a burst of breath extinguishing invisible fires around me. These days, in my more spiritual moments, I often feel the fire burning in my soul, but the words still work their magic, though only sometimes.

Martin said he had had enough of the field and now wanted the boring security of a job in the office. Field of course was the name of the town we lived in, but I guess he was referring to the fields of fire. I couldn't seem to understand then what he was getting at. It was only later that I began to see 'field' as some place where you work more with your hands than your mind, quite different from an office where the mind becomes more important than hands.

Within days of arriving in Warsaw we moved from our room in the hotel to an airy, spacious apartment not far from the city centre. The really neat thing about the apartment was that it also came with a girl-friend that I had so much wished for Martin. She was absolutely stunning. My father had not forewarned me about her, so I was somewhat indifferent as I stood outside the apartment door with our suitcases and bags and rang the bell. What did this new situation hold for me? This new home in this new city where the only place I knew so far was the railway station which stood directly in front of our hotel and a beautiful monument called the Palace of Culture which stood alongside the station. I had never seen anything like it before. It was prettier than the many needle-like towers back home. Over time, I grew to think of the 'palace' as the ugliest building in the entire city.

In my nervousness, as we stood in front of our new apartment, I started to whisper *Adair, Adair*, wishing for good things to happen to us. Something inside me prompted me to mutter the name like a chant. And there she was. At first I was shocked, but soon my joy was boundless when I realized that she was to be a mother to me as well. I decided then and there that I would henceforth use *Adair, Adair* as a personal charm. It seemed to be working like magic for me. I, Matthew, loved the idea, although I was careful not to use the chant for frivolous reasons. Over time, however, the subject of chanting *Adair, Adair* would turn out to be the first serious difference of view between Misha and me. Misha lived for the moment and had little use for delving into the past to shape the future. The name Adair meant nothing to him.

This was Lydia, and after she had kissed my father it was my turn to be pressed against her breast and kissed over and over again like a darling pet. Something inside of me thrilled to the name Misha, which she kept muttering under her breath, but what I liked even more was the amazing perfume she wore. I had never known anything like it. The closest I had come to experiencing such fragrance was in the cosmetics section of the large department stores. Of course, it was quite different there, like a disconnected sound floating in the air around which you cannot conjure a human voice or a human face. Lydia was something else. I decided it would be more appropriate to think of her in terms of a garden or a flower shop where one might sniff and stare and sometimes fondle some things in one's fingers. And that's what I'll think forever.

"You will be my Misha," she said. I kissed her back. It was as if we were sealing a pact, a kind of sworn bonding - as I heard the shrinks saying more than once - that I had never had with my biological mother.

The image of my mother has been chiselled in my memory for a long time. It is not a nice image. My mother strapped to a bed, hoarse whispers escaping her lips as she jerked her head off the pillow from time to time, a pleading look in her eyes. Her eyes, and the closely cropped head of jet-black hair, are the only dark objects I remember in an otherwise spotlessly white bed and white-painted room with off-white floors. One day, there was this plump, red-faced man, also wearing a white coat and white trousers, who bent forward and jabbed a needle in mother's arm. Then she was quiet.

This sad memory of my mother began to fade gradually during the first happy days, weeks, months in our apartment on Akademicka, a quiet street where diplomats and business-men habitually came looking for young companions. There was this fragrance hanging in the air wherever Lydia went. Now that I think of it, it was never the same. Lavender, jasmine, roses - I was never very good with flowers except the common ones - but, yes, the fragrance was different from day to day. Then there was this wonderful smell of cooked food. Suddenly, my life was changed. Living with my father meant that we ate a lot of quick barbecues, frozen pizza and other pre-cooked food which I imagined being prepared in enormous vats, stirred by mechanical arms and zapped by lasers and chemicals. We also ate a lot at fast-food outlets. After a while, they all tasted the same. Good maybe, but the same. Lydia brought real excitement surging through my stomach at mealtimes each day. Even the aroma of her soups was something that gives me goose-pimples for thinking to this day. In moments like these, both Matthew and Misha were starry-eyed about her.

If one had to go by what Mr. Kerrigan believed, my mother had no choice but to become the strange creature that she did. Church people in Field might think God was punishing my mother for some unspeakable sins, but Mr. Kerrigan was kinder. He thought that was a lot of nonsense. The facts apparently were that the seeds of my mother's madness were planted the moment the egg that produced my mother was fertilized in my grandmother's womb by my grandfather's sperm. Pretty complicated stuff when you think how simple it is to start the works. To tell you the truth, I really didn't know whom to believe, but Mr. Kerrigan has been quite persuasive.

Sometimes I wonder whether a mother isn't like a lottery. You are never sure what you might come up with. I had had two shots at the lottery for mothers, coming up empty-handed the first time. A little better the second time around. I was stuck with one father and I'm never sure whether I came up a winner or a loser. What was it like to hit the jackpot with one's parents? Great looking parents who live in freshly painted cottages with manicured lawns and spotless kitchens, who drive shiny cars and holiday in Mediterranean and Caribbean resorts. Since I don't know anyone who has done so, the matter remains a mystery to me.

I keep thinking Martin Fisher was probably born to fight fires. No sooner had he settled down to his oil-based desk job in Warsaw, he was off once again capping blown oil wells and fighting oil fires in some sea or desert or God knows where else. At school I tried to keep track of his travels by noting his destinations against a large globe. I would imagine myself trudging through tropical jungles, mesmerized by the eyes of a tiger or a snake. I pictured myself riding a camel on the desert sands, wearing the shimmering white robes of Peter O'Toole as Lawrence of Arabia. But I soon lost interest in these daydreams. My father's absences became more and more frequent, and he was gone for longer and longer periods. I never saw him actually fight with Lydia, but I overheard some fearful arguments when he came home from his travels. In the end, I always found Lydia crying her heart out all by herself. It was obvious they were not getting along at all, and I know Misha began to worry for himself. We were beginning to like the new country and even knew a little of its new language. The prospect of moving again began to look quite depressing.

Martin always left money with Lydia for my needs, as he told me every time we said good-bye. Soon I didn't mind him going away. Sometimes, I half hoped he would never come back because I got to sleep with Lydia when he was away. What I felt in bed with her was probably what people feel when they are drunk. I have been drunk a few times and that's why I can say this. It was as if my body and my mind had changed into a musical instrument and I was like the strings of a harp. And somebody was playing me like in a concert. I had become the music, and the breeze blew the perfume from her body like it was my music's echo.

"Why do you leave Lydia and go away so often?" I once asked, and was promptly rewarded with a tight slap across my face. I leapt back in surprise and started to whimper. The stinging pain I felt refused to go away until Lydia had smothered me in her arms and overwhelmed me with her perfume. To this day, I cannot understand what I had done wrong, why I deserved to be slapped by my father.

In spite of all that had happened, I kept hoping that Matthew and Martin might someday grow to respect one another. But I never had any doubt of the deep love between Misha and his mother. Still, when I asked her for eighty nine zlotys to buy a pair of new Adidas I had seen on sale in the Central Station arcade, I was stunned by the sternness of her refusal. I didn't think I was asking for anything out of the ordinary, since most of my belongings were of a rather good quality. I seemed to dress better than most of my fellow students at school. Our apartment overlooked a large, sometimes scary, park and was rather nice, much nicer than the dark old-fashioned places my friends lived in. Lydia herself, as far as I could tell, was not only the most beautiful woman in the city but also the best-dressed. The last pair of shoes she brought home cost her twice as much as the Adidas I needed. So what was the problem?

She must have seen the look of disappointment on my face, for she immediately put her arms round me and said I should probably go to the stadium on the other side of the river and buy a pair from the foreign vendors who had driven out all the local traders from the area.

"But you know very well the Russians will cheat me," I reminded her.

"Why shouldn't they?" she asked, a big smile on her face. "Your dad cheated me and went off to Siberia, didn't he? Sometimes I hope his bones are rotting somewhere in the vast icefields."

One part of me readily joined in her laughter. The other me began to feel guilty soon afterwards. Having hardly seen or spent time with Martin - or so it was beginning to seem to me these past few months - it made little difference whether his bones were rotting in the icefields or, as Lydia would propose at other times, in hell. Misha often wondered what fathers were needed for. Oh! Matthew is not so innocent that I don't know about that. I haven't studied genes for nothing. You know what I mean. Once that is over and done with, what good is a father? My friends have fathers who sometimes cheer them on at soccer. My mother does the same for me. Some fathers I know drive expensive new cars. We don't have a car, but mother and I can go wherever we want to in taxis, or our friends drive us to the lakes or to the ski slopes on weekends. As for carrying large parcels, I have helped Lydia with the shopping for as long as I can remember.

When Mr. Mansell comes to visit Lydia on his business trips from abroad, he always makes me sit on his lap, messes up my hair, and says how I could easily pass for his son. "Such gorgeous black eyes," he says every time. "Such rich black hair." If I liked Mr. Mansell it's not because he said such nice things about my hair, but because he never forgot to bring me his customary four bars of Mars chocolates from wherever. I don't think I would care to have him as a father. What good would he be? Besides, he ought to do something about the terrible smell of garlic on his breath, I thought. Drove me crazy, and I couldn't even run away from his lap because of the chocolates he had brought me. As for my eyes and hair, the girls in the orphanage told me that all the time, every time one of them pulled me into a closet for some simmering passion. I'd never have known how much fun they have in the orphanage had two of my street acquaintances not introduced me to their friends. Now, these orphanage boys and girls have neither fathers nor mothers, but they have a lot of fun just the same. I doubt if I could do without my mother, but a father ..... Who cares? Marek, of course, had totally different notions of orphanages.

One-Three

I saw no reason to pretend I was different from the other kids. To others, I was Misha, exactly as my mother had registered me at school. They would ask me where I was before I came to Warsaw. "Oh! here and there," I'd say, "everywhere my father's work took him to." But I was not permitted to say where, because that was the nature of my father's work. No, he was not a spy. No, he was not a gangster.

But the eyes and the hair caused me no end of trouble sometimes. During the first two years in my new school off Wawelska, I did not have a single friend. That wouldn't have been so bad if I wasn't bullied and kicked all the time. Almost everyday I'd go home in tears. Sometimes I'd have cuts and bruises; at other times, my clothes would be torn or muddied. It was Lydia who pointed me in the right direction one day. "Can't you get some help from one of the bigger boys?" she asked. That's when I turned to Stanislaus, in the same class as me and by far one of the toughest boys in school. Stanislaus was clever and, much to my surprise, somewhat younger than me. At first I was a bit diffident about approaching him. Eventually, I told him what was happening to me and the kind of help my mother had asked me to look for.

"You think they're after you because of your skin?" asked Stan.

"Perhaps," I replied. I looked at my arms, my hands, and realized that in summer I might look about the same as the others, but there was no mistaking my darker complexion in the winter when the sun only rarely showed its face through the clouds of coal dust and other fumes sitting over the city.

"Maybe it's your hair and eyes," continued Stan.

"Maybe."

"Tell you what. If anyone ever asks you about your hair, tell them your hair got charred, at the moment of your birth, from the fire in your mother's loins."

"And my eyes?" I asked, not quite certain what Stan was talking about.

"The same with the eyes," said Stan. "The fire in her womb. It would've blinded you for life if you had lighter eyes, you stinking Jew."

I thought it was a joke, and laughed. Of course, I was anything but a Jew. It was only much later that I understood what Stan was trying to tell me. It became obvious that he had seen my mother and was inflamed by her beauty. Fortunately, I didn't have to offer Stan's explanation to anyone. Word travelled pretty quickly that anyone laying his hands on me would be answerable to Stan. From that day, nobody touched me. But I soon realized that every favour, however small, has its price. Stan didn't ask for much. Only, once in a while he would take off his pants and want me to play with him. I didn't mind, since it seemed far more convenient than being spat upon and pushed into gutters.

The Adidas took hold of my mind in such a way that I began to devise the most improbable schemes for getting them. But I stayed clear of *Adair, Adair* this time. Instead, I thought of going to a store, putting on a new pair pretending to try them on, then dashing out of the store into the crowd outside. It would have to be in the evening, with people rushing home from work. But it wasn't any good. It wouldn't work. I finally decided to settle for even an used pair, if necessary. But I certainly wasn't going to buy any cheap imitation from the

Russian peasants across the river. Instead, I thought of finding someone with my size of shoes, of fairly good condition naturally, waiting for a tram. At the right moment, I would push him onto the tracks in front of a running tram. After that, it would be a simple matter to take off his shoes when he was either dead or unconscious. Then I became worried to think the person might really die. There'd be no end of trouble for me. I, Matthew, dropped the idea almost as quickly as Misha had thought about it.

It was Stan once again who came to the rescue. "Why don't you try and earn some extra money like the rest of us. If I didn't like you, I'd ask you to sell these pills," he said, pulling out a small plastic container from his pocket and rattling the white pills inside in my face. "You'd get caught and land us all in shit."

Instead, what Stan proposed was that I go to work evenings for one of the few elderly Jews who still remained in the city. One saw them, but only rarely, in the public gardens and the open markets. It was easy to spot them because they always looked so terrified, and dressed in clothes that had gone out of fashion fifty years ago. Most of them lived in apartments near a dark stone memorial to the dead, and it was there one Sunday morning that I went pressing doorbells and asking if there was any work for a young boy of thirteen.

Stan had warned me, "They're shit scared of people. So be prepared for a lot of no's." I pressed along from door to door, each time rehearsing a new set of lines to open the conversation. Of the sixty odd buzzers that I pressed, almost half didn't even bother to reply. The others all said there was nothing for me. I was starting to give up hope, but kept muttering *Adair, Adair* with increasing intensity until one call brought a surprising response. After pressing the buzzer I gave my usual pitch, somewhat half-hearted by this time, without even waiting for a voice to ask me who I was or what I wanted. Strangely, the person at the other end released the entrance lock. But I heard no one's voice. I was so taken aback that I couldn't open the door in time. What's worse, I even forgot the apartment number I was buzzing. I thought I had pressed a buzzer marked 'Rubinstein', so I pressed it once more. Again, a voiceless presence at the other end opened the lock for me. This time I knew where to go.

I climbed up a single flight of stairs and was in front of number fifteen. I could see the door was slightly open but felt a little nervous about pushing it further and walking in. Moments later, someone pulled open the door from the inside and I stood facing a tall, skinny man with a beard which looked like it had been worked over with a hedge cutter. A few grey tufts of hair lined his bald head which was shaped almost like a peaked cap. I had a chance to notice all this, as well as his somewhat shabby clothes because he didn't utter a word as we stood facing each other. He had a stick in his hand, and his eyes were quite expressionless. They were peaceful eyes, and I could see right away he was blind. His hand moved slowly to his chest and it was then that I noticed he had a piece of slate hanging by a thread around his neck. He wrote on this slate: "What can you do for me?"

Great, I thought to myself as I realized the man had no voice.

There was a moment when I thought I didn't want to have anything to do with this Rubinstein. But he turned his face to me as if straining to catch my voice. So I said, simply, "Anything." I stood there facing him, not knowing what more to say. I could sense Misha liked him too. It didn't seem fair to have him write when others could simply move their lips in reply. It was fairer to remain silent. Rubenstein seemed lost in thought for several moments. Then he wrote something else on his slate and held it up for me. He had written: "Tagore?"

I stared at the word for a long time, then looked up at the man for some clues. I was lost. Finally, I said, "I don't know what you mean." Mr. Rubinstein smiled, shrugged his bony shoulders, and I imagined the matter would end there.

But the word stuck in my mind. "Tagore?" I asked myself on my way home the first night. It seemed odd that Mr. Rubinstein should bring up that word during the first few moments of our meeting. What was it? What did the word mean? Was it something bad that people did to others, something I hadn't heard about? My instinct led me to ask Stan first. He was pretty good with words and seemed most knowledgeable about these things. Stan thought about it all morning and finally told me during the lunch recess. "It's a funny word and I can't seem to figure it out at all. You don't suppose it's something kinky from the Hebrew bible, that he wants to gore you, or something?"

I hadn't thought of that possibility. I must admit that the prospect of being gored was a little alarming, but I quickly dismissed the thought as I couldn't see a blind old man proving any threat to me.

I wasn't sure how Martin would react to the idea of his son going to work after school for a blind Jewish nobody. Maybe he would feel obligated to give him some more pocket-money so he didn't have to do it. On the other hand, there was the possibility of a certain loss of face with Stan if he didn't. "These old Jews are real suckers," he said. "Once you gain their confidence, you can do very well indeed." So I decided to stick it out as long as I could.

While our first encounter was pleasant enough, I soon discovered a darker, irritable, and cantankerous side to Marek, the name by which he asked me to address him from the very beginning. While it often took him a few moments to write his questions or instructions on the slate, he seemed to expect, even demand, an almost immediate response from me. If he didn't get it, perhaps because I hadn't noticed him writing or couldn't immediately figure out what he had written, he would start thumping on the table, a book, the side of a chair, or whatever was handy in order to attract my attention. I soon got used to this after a couple of days.

The first evening was quite uneventful. He walked around the apartment with me, showing me where he kept his books, his writing material, his groceries, his tobacco and cigarette paper. It was easy enough, for the apartment wasn't very big. But I ran into another of his eccentricities when I took him out for a walk the next evening. He seemed to have a good idea of the ins and outs of his neighbourhood and was quite precise about which streets he wanted to be on and which he wanted to avoid. But the problem arose when, every twenty or thirty steps he would stop and write on his slate: "Big kids around?" or "Men, grown-ups or young?" He generally took care to erase the words as soon as I had answered, but sometimes he left the words on the slate and simply stopped me and pointed to them.

Often, there were kids, boisterous ones, up ahead. Marek would simply have me cross over to the other side of the street or wait. I could sense the fear rising in him as I held his hand. Finally, I couldn't help saying, "You don't seem to like kids and young men."

"They've been the bane of our life these last few years," he wrote angrily on his slate.

"How come you let me take you around?" I asked.

Marek stopped in his tracks. I saw the lines on his face softening somewhat. He even smiled as he wrote, "You've got to have faith in something."

Our conversation was slow and circuitous, and there were times I seriously wondered if it was all worth it. I knew I would have enough to buy my shoes by the end of three weeks, but after the first week I was even less enthusiastic about the Adidas than I was about my job.

The third day, Lydia came over with me to check out the area. Misha couldn't understand her concern for what was obviously my safety. "You seem to be afraid something terrible might happen to me," I said to her. Lydia replied that the Jewish part of the city was never a nice place. "I'm not Jewish," I protested.

She thought it was just as bad that I was working for a Jew. "But I can't help it," I said. "Where else am I going to find work?" It seemed to settle the issue when I told her Stan had suggested I look for this kind of a job. Ultimately, she decided the section of town wasn't as crime-ridden as she had thought. But Lydia should've worn something other than her short leather skirt, a flaming red blouse and black stilettos. Her dress and the attention it was beginning to attract made me quite nervous. She could well have brought muggers out of hiding and started a crime wave in the neighbourhood, I thought.

By now I was quite familiar with Marek's apartment and his possessions. As might be expected, his books intrigued me. There were numerous books on religion and, miraculously, it was among his books that I found the clue to Tagore. There seemed to be as many books by him as there were books about him. While I remained curious as to why he had asked me about Tagore the very first day, I decided not to bring up the subject for the present. The books simply didn't arouse my curiosity.

Meanwhile, there was no news from Martin Fisher. He had completed his Siberian assignment and had moved on to an off-shore platform in the North Sea. "So much for his office job," I remember grumbling over dinner. I suspect I was half hoping he would come home and put an end to the idea of working for Marek. From time to time, Lydia would sulk over the idea. I don't think she really wanted me to go to work for Marek Rubinstein. Still, I feel Lydia didn't seem to mind my absences after school. I think she even preferred it that way. She always left me something in the fridge, except on weekends when we usually dined together. There was always a bowl of goulash or some potato pancakes or a slice of pizza at other times.

One-Four

"Keep everything, don't throw away a single scrap of paper," Connie called out to me from the sofa. "They'll make you rich someday."

Rudely awakened, I replied loudly that I had no intentions of throwing away any of Marek's papers. She seemed more engrossed in reading than in putting books away. But we were in no hurry, and I saw no need to prod her. I wanted the hours to drag on.

"I'm working, I'm working," she reassured me with a smile.

I was working too, but her smile and the nearness of her glorious body, now glistening with points of light reflecting off tiny beads of perspiration, began to prove too distracting. I noticed a shortness of breath and a hardening of the anatomy, both of which seemed quite incompatible with physical labour. I looked at myself, somewhat covered with the grime and dust we had awakened from their rest between old letters and even older books, and decided against entwining my limbs with Connie's just then. It would've been in bad taste. "I'm going for a bath," I said, "and then I'm taking a break."

"Good idea," she replied, without taking her eyes off from whatever she was reading.

The bathtub looked clean enough. Connie told me how it had to be scrubbed repeatedly with hospital strength detergent after they had fished Marek's body out of it. I remembered I had brought Marek several packets of bath gel from Lydia's endless horde collected from her excursions of love into the Marriott Hotel's numerous guest rooms. While I ran the water, I decided to look for them. I found them exactly where I had stashed them, in a corner of the medicine cabinet. Marek seemed to have had no use for them.

The bath water bubbled slightly and gave off a warm, inviting fragrance. It took an age to fill, so I plunged in and began to scrub myself with soap. I had half a mind to call Connie to scrub my back, but there was already so much dark scum in the bathtub that I decided against calling her. Instead, I quickly completed the scrubbing and let the water drain out.

"What, finished already?" Connie cried out, as she heard the last of the water gurgling through the vent.

"Oh, no. I'm just getting ready for the real thing."

"Good. Don't rush."

When the warm water filled up the bathtub quite nicely once again, and the contents of another Marriott bath gel had perfumed the air, I closed my eyes and wondered how beautiful it would be to end my life just then. A glorious end for both Matthew and Misha, in one fell swoop. I hoped Marek, lying exactly where I was now lying, had felt he same way, the same sense of gladness and contentment, and that he had been able to freeze the moment as it were into his eternity. It didn't seem strange that these thoughts were floating through my mind as if on a cloud of memory because, moments earlier, I had been thinking of the books Connie was arranging. And I was thinking I should ask her to set aside Tagore's plays for me. After what Marek had told us, I was quite keen to read "The Post Office", a precious volume of which I know lay among Marek's books. Tagore seemed to be talking of death, although Marek didn't quite agree with what he was saying. To be thinking these thoughts, I again realized I was getting old for my years. But who, Matthew or Misha? And suddenly the question didn't seem all that important. Finally, I had to ask her, "Have you come to the Tagore plays?"

"Not yet."

"Do set aside "The Post Office" for me when you find it. I'd like to read it, and not have to go through all the boxes to find it. It could be just a sheaf of papers written in his own hand."

"Sure."

I drifted back to my dream-like state. I heard occasional faint sounds coming from Connie's room, but they seemed incapable of awakening me. But then I suddenly smelt something, something quite different from the bath gel. Could it be gas, I wondered in my half-sleep. It was stupid of me to think of gas, because gas had probably never smelt like incense.

"Is that incense?" I cried out from the bath. It took a great deal of effort to shout the words. I had to form them in my mind for quite some time before I could give voice to them.

"Yes, I bought some yesterday. Forgot to empty my bag."

"How convenient." Then I quickly added, because Connie knew I was sensitive to smells, "I like it."

Peace and quiet descended on my bathtub once more. I thought I could hear voices singing. Suddenly the voices rose, a chorus charged with devotion. The organ pealed a few heavenly notes. "What's that?" I cried, with as much alarm as exhaustion.

"Bach," she cried back.

"Where did he come from?" I simply couldn't help asking, "Your bag as well?"

"Oh, no. It's one of Marek's tapes. *Jesu, meine Freude.*"

Actually, the music and the incense had the remarkable effect of quietly sending me back to my half-sleep world of softly parading thoughts. But I was in for another rude shock.

Suddenly, I felt a kiss, a gentle, chaste kiss on my lips. Startled, even though the carefully calibrated pressure of the lips on my own seemed in perfect harmony with Bach in the background, I opened my eyes to see Connie smiling in my face. "That was meant to signal an awakening of desire. In me that is," she quickly added.

In another time and place, that information would be exciting and welcome news. But covered upto my neck in bathwater, all I could bring myself to say was, "What's going on?"

"Well, I've been reading this splendid book on love. What a treasure Marek has left for you. It's pure science. Let me see whether you're a rabbit, a bull, or a horse." With that, she grabbed my penis and yanked it out of the water. I almost jumped out of my skin, but in reality half the bath-water splashed out of the tub and on the floor. That didn't seem to distract Connie who now proceeded to measure my penis with her fingers. "Six or seven index fingers," she reflected thoughtfully. "Perhaps you're only a rabbit." She tightened her grip on my shell-shocked limb -'pudenda' according to the book, she said - although neither of us had any idea what the word meant. "Too bad, ten fingers and you'd have been a bull; twelve, a horse." She nodded her head ruefully and sighed.

By now, I was gaining control over my senses. Or becoming acutely aware of them, I should say. "What would you have wished for?" I asked.

"Oh! I don't know. I'm not fussy." She let go of me and stood up, spreading her legs wide apart in the process. She peered down, or so it seemed, deep into her groin and said, "I suppose that depends largely on what I am myself - a deer, a mare, or a she-elephant."

"Definitely not a she-elephant," I said. "Can't you find out?"

"Well, the instructions aren't very clear on the subject, not half as clear as with cocks. It says here it's a matter of fit. A good tight fit with you would make me a deer, although I can't imagine a deer and a rabbit screwing one another. If you disappear and get lost inside me, you'd still be the rabbit but I'd be a mare.

"How was I the last time you fitted me out?" I asked.

"That's the trouble. I don't remember. I wasn't paying attention."

I wasn't about to waste any more time. Although I didn't really care who it was I pleased - Matthew or Misha - there's no question that a part of me simply adores scientific evidence. "Let's find out," I said, as I pulled Connie into the bathtub. While she didn't resist me, she allowed herself to slide across my body to one side of the tub. The water level rose immediately and seemed to work wonders for my rabbit prick. "Look how it's grown," I said."

"Yes, but it also looks bent and crooked."

"That's parallax," I said.

"You're only a growing boy," she said as she held my face in both her hands and started to nibble on my ear.

I lay on my back while she quickened her thrusts into me, and I felt myself drowning and I loved every moment of it. I finally died, and the bubbles that rose from my body weren't bubbles of air coming from my mouth. It was my flesh and blood that spilled into her, seared her soft inside until she whimpered and cried, then rose like bubbles and floated to the surface as she slid out of me and lay down beside me in the tub. All the while, Bach played on.

When I finally regained my breath, I told her, "The experiment was a total failure."

"Yes." She sounded disappointed, but I knew she was pretending. "The principal author doesn't approve of love-making in water, but others encourage it as a pleasant diversion."

"Did they suggest incense and music?"

"Oh yes," she was quick to reply, "and much more. Like greenery and flowers and fresh, clean linen. And a silk dress for me, and stimulating drinks and refreshments."

"I know where we went wrong," I said, remembering the champagne and the cheese and baguettes. "What is this book?" I asked, as I put on one of Marek's fresh shirts and tossed one to Connie. I made sure Connie's was made of silk.

"It's a translation. It's called Maharshi Vatsyayana's 'Kama Sutra'. It's a famous ancient Indian classic of love."

"Jesus Christ, where has it been hiding all these years?" I asked.

"Where else, but in Marek's book-shelf," she said, slowly articulating each word, playfully nodding her head. "Too hot for anywhere else."

"So what are you, a deer or a mare?"

"We'll do it right this time, step by step," she replied. "Let's get the food out first."

So we laid out the table, setting up two places facing each other. Connie brought out the cheese and salami, while I set two wine glasses, there being no champagne glasses in the unpretentious crockery cabinet. While she was slicing the bread, I picked up the frail paperback. On the cover was the picture of some kind of a fat deity. Inside, there were a half dozen pictures of ancient sculptures, well-endowed men and women embracing each other. Nothing earth-shattering. I loved the dedication on the inside front cover : To all healthy young men and women in India and abroad who seek continual amorous pleasures and everlasting happiness in their married life, this treatise is chivalrously presented. "Hey!" I cried. "Wonder if this book is available only in sex shops. It's for married couples."

"Don't you believe it," said Connie, snatching the book away from my hands. "It tells you how and when to screw your friends' wives, servant girls, the lot." Reading from the pages now, she said, "There are seven varieties of screwing - wholehearted passion (that must be us), inspired passion (us too, I guess), transferred passion (when you're screwing someone and thinking of someone else), libido passion (what you do to servants and whores), secret passion (discreetly, with your mistress), spontaneous (suddenly it happens), and artificial (when you must pretend, because your heart isn't in it, like when you're a gigolo).

"You've certainly picked up a lot in an afternoon's reading."

She ignored my jibe and said, "This seating isn't right." Flipping through the pages quickly, she came to a spot and stopped. "It says here that I am to sit on your right so you can embrace me with your right hand and pour the drinks with your left." We re-arranged the seating to accommodate Vatsyayana. The incense still hung in the air. For music, we decided to skip Bach and turned to the radio instead. After a few minutes of head-banging rock, however softly played, we decided to do away with the music.

We smiled a lot while we bit off pieces of bread. I plied her with an excessive amount of bubbly. I touched her nipples softly, felt the warmth in her thighs, all using the right hand as recommended. "You're supposed to be saying, 'very delicious,' 'very sweet,' 'very saltish,' 'very spicy' and such other nice compliments," she reminded me. In all fairness to what we were eating, all I could come up with was 'very delicious', and 'very saltish' with respect to the cheese. After a while, we got tired of the niceties.

But we did make love as we had never done before. She showed me her cunt while she sat on the bed, her legs spread out and bent at the knees. "What does it look like?" she asked. I had no answer for her. To think I had never really seen a woman's cunt. "It should look like a lotus flower," she said.

"It does, it does," I replied. "The petals folded so gently at the top."

"It should resemble a flame rising from a lamp."

"It does, it does," I repeated, feeling the soothing heat on my face.

"Look closer, and you'll see a tiny seed. Take it between your lips as you would an offering in the house of God."

I crushed my face between her legs until my tears of joy become one with her ocean surging into my mouth. It was as if I had entered a secret grotto and was overcome by a numbing mysticism. She clung to me like a vine, she climbed me like a tree, she pounced upon me like a tiger. Then she spun around me like a wheel, my burning penis an axle of fire. She spun and she spun and she spun, and the fire spread to every part of my body and I was reduced to dust and ashes.

Afterwards, she made me sit on her left as before, and had me pour out a single glass of champagne. "I'll drink half of it," she said, reaching for the glass, "and you'll drink the other half." And she lifted my hand to her breast and showed me how to leave on her skin the mark of a peacock's foot - my nails making a curved mark on her white skin, the red flashes converging on her nipples. I mounted her when we made love soon afterwards. She held herself like a crab, her supple feet planted on her stomach, while I floundered against her legs resisting me like a brick wall. Quite inadvertently, I scratched her from her left nipple right up to her neck. Afterwards, she looked at it with delight and said it was a 'tiger's claw'. Then we sat and watched the moon rise over the park while a German station played Duke Ellington on the radio. Before the evening had gone too far, we tried the yawning position with her feet mounted on my shoulders. That felt good, although I couldn't resist telling her it felt like I was entering a she-elephant from the classification list. She said the problem was mine, not hers, and added, as if to make her point, "You rabbit." But when it came to doing the split bamboo, I had had enough. I had to beg off because of a real fear that my penis might get detached from my body. Connie took it all in good humour, although she thought the book suggested that she should show some displeasure at my incapacity. But looking up the book for such a minor detail didn't seem worth the bother.

That sustained physical activity gives rise to a healthy appetite soon became evident as we both made individual forays to the fridge and found nothing that would satisfy either of us. There was a bottle of wine and some beer, both of which seemed quite anti-climactic after what we had been through. "Man does not live by flesh alone," Lydia was fond of saying, but she said it only to bolster her case for a vegetarian diet, nothing else. Connie's and my appetites both began to crave for some meat at this moment, but somehow we felt too tired to dress beyond Marek's shirts which had stood a lot of wear for a single afternoon. At the very least, we had firmly established that a silk shirt plays an important role in love-making.

One-Five

A sudden knock on the door quickly forced us back to reality. Who could it be, I wondered as I slipped into my trousers. Connie stepped into the bedroom to get dressed. It was Tetsuo. He had known that we would be in the apartment cleaning up. "I brought some flowers," he said, "because Marek loved them." I took the flowers from him and placed them in a bowl. Tetsuo walked around. First to the writing desk where I had bunches of papers and letters clipped together or tied with rubber bands. He looked at them in silence for a moment or two. "Where's Connie?" he asked, moving towards the empty bookshelves.

"She's getting dressed," I said.

Tetsuo stopped in front of the window. "So you've been working hard," he said, tapping on the topmost of the five boxes Connie had filled up with Marek's books.

"Hot and dusty work," I said.

"Yes, it's been a warm day," he replied, picking up a solitary book Connie had left on the window table. "The Post Office," he said. "Hnh!"

"Marek loved the play," I said.

"I know," replied Tetsuo as Connie came and joined us. She smiled at Tetsuo and stood near us. Tetsuo's sharp eyes seemed to be taking note of the ravages of recent ecstasy on her face. He paused an instant and continued, "I'm sorry I have been such a cad with Marek's script. I had promised him I would marry the words, if only he'd write them down, to the music flowing through his mind, the music I happened to be holding in my hands. I should've known the idea as unrealisable, perhaps even unwholesome, and let it fly past like a summer's cloud. But I didn't. I kept pretending I would

43

someday make good on my promise. I was not true to myself, and now I am full of remorse."

"No harm was done, Tetsuo," said Connie, moving closer and slipping her arm around his. Tetsuo didn't look up, didn't flinch. He seemed lost in contemplation of the book, its simple cover with the name of the play and the author, Rabindranath Tagore. The translator's name wasn't on the cover.

"Could we read it sometime?" he asked. "The three of us."

"Sure," replied Connie, "if it'll make you feel any better."

"It will," he said. "Can we do it tonight?"

Connie and I looked at each other. Connie was the first to speak. "Perhaps," she said, "but we need something to eat first."

"Certainly, be my guest," said Tetsuo. He was always most gracious with entertainment, and did not disappoint us that night as we drove in his car to the Old Town. We parked and walked over to his favourite restaurant, Fukier. Everybody knew him there, and they knew us too.

As usual, Mr. Gessler brought Connie a bunch of beautiful roses and bowed as he gave them to her. She looked absolutely radiant as she held them close to her and breathed the fragrance. "Where have you been all these months, years?" Mr. Gessler asked me. "Haven't seen you in ages."

"You have a great memory," I said, adding, "I've been in prison."

Mr. Gessler kept on smiling, pretending he hadn't heard me. The music had been playing even as we entered. Now it grew louder as the musicians advanced in our direction. The food and the music brought the afternoon back to me like the softness of a cool moist breeze reaching inwards to wipe pain and tears troubling the heart. We had music too, and food, and lots of loving. Would it be he same if we were to repeat the afternoon in Fukier? I didn't pursue the question very far in my mind. And I couldn't take my eyes off Connie.

"What is it about the play that so affected Marek?" asked Tetsuo, as he drove us back home. "And the music he wanted so badly as an accompaniment to the words....it was wierd. He said he had heard it for the past fifty years. And I know for a fact Gorecki wrote it only a few years ago."

"I don't know," I said, "it's very strange." Which was an honest answer because I too had thought about the question while in prison, but never really tried to put the pieces together for an answer. From the way Marek had meticulously described it to me, it was the same music that has been playing in my mind, God knows how long.

"So you want us to go through with the reading tonight?" asked Connie.

"You're not tired, are you?" he asked, turning to look at her.

"Not really," she lied.

"Well, just a fragment maybe. Then we'll see."

Both Connie and I felt we owed Tetsuo the reading, not because of the dinner he had treated us to, but because of what had happened earlier. From the ridiculous to the sublime, or maybe the other way round? I had no idea. "Shall I get some wine?" I asked, once back in the apartment.

"I'll pass," said Tetsuo.

"I'd love some," said Connie as she settled in the middle of the sofa. Since we had only one book, we decided she should sit in the middle with it, and that we would take turns with the voices. I pushed a floor lamp in front of Connie and switched off the main lights. The darkness surrounding our little space on the sofa looked like an outpouring of the shadows that lay outside the window. Somehow, it presented us with the illusion that we were an island, a small world all to ourselves, and that we were communicating with another world stretching from the confines of the room to the boundaries of space unconquered even by the imagination.

"I think Marek would've loved us doing this," suggested Connie.

"I think he's listening in," said Tetsuo. I thought so too.

"Let's begin," said Connie.

The opening lines of the play belonged to a character called Madhav. "How shall we manage the voices?" I asked.

"Make each voice our own, taking turns," suggested Tetsuo, "and let's not overlook the stage directions."

As we started, the wind rose suddenly. The sound of the wind through the window was like a choir of mournful voices singing. We looked at each other silently, puzzled, and started.

* * * *

Madhav: [looking worried and confused]: *This has got to stop. This is not his home, and yet it is.*

I can't figure out what's going on. I'm a stranger in my own house. But no stranger to him.

So why do I suffer so?

Physician: *He lives, if he must. He dies, if he will. I have no cures. I can only offer straws that people cling to, for a while.*

Madhav: *Is there anything I can do?*

Physician: *Very little. Keep him inside if you can.*

Madhav: *He's a child. You can't lock up a child indoors. How am I to do that?*

Physician: *Like you lock up anyone else. Bolt the doors.*

Madhav: *Strong medicine, eh?*

Physician: *That's the only kind that works. The make-*
             believe ones work the best.

             [Exit Physician]

             [Enter Bearded Neighbour]

Madhav: *I wish you weren't here.*

Neighbour: *But why?*

Madhav: *You upset kids. You drive them crazy.*

Neighbour: *So what's the problem. You have no children.*

Madhav: *Now I do. My wife wanted a child so badly,*
             I've had to adopt this boy.

Neighbour: *I know she has been dying to adopt. But you*
             never liked the idea. What good are children,
             anyway?

Madhav: *All this around me, my possessions. I've*
             worked so hard to earn it all. Couldn't bear
             the thought of everything passing to a
             stranger. But this orphan lad has nothing,
             and I'll be happy to leave everything to him.

Neighbour: *I can see your precious logic. So why do you*
             look upset?

Madhav: *The child is very ill. The physician thinks the*
             autumn winds will make him worse.

             So I must keep him indoors, rested. If he sees
             you, he'll jump out of bed and want to play.

Neighbour: *Dear me! I'd better be going. I'll see him later*
             perhaps.

             [Exit Neighbour]

We had run out of the three voices that we made up, and now we had come to Amal. We looked around for a fourth. Connie picked up the cue, doubling as Amal's voice. The wind meanwhile had become stronger, and the mournful strains louder.

[Enter Amal]

Amal: *Hello Uncle! I do want to go outside so badly.*

Madhav: *I'm afraid you can't. You heard what the doctor said.*

Amal: *There's a squirrel out there sitting with his tail up, watching mother grind the lentils.*

           Can't I go as far as the squirrel?

Madhav: *Sorry. You know what the doctor'll say.*

Amal: *Wouldn't it be fun if I were a squirrel? But tell me, does the doctor know everything?*

           His books, do they teach him everything?

Madhav: *The great scholars are a bit like you. They never go out. They've eyes only for books.*

           I think you'll probably be a great teacher when you grow up. You'll read big books, difficult books, and tell everyone what ideas lie hidden in them.

Amal: *Not really. I'm not too keen on learning. I'd rather go out and see everything there is.*

           I want to go beyond those hills. Do you know something? Yesterday I met someone who was just as crazy about those hills. He had a bamboo staff on his shoulder with a small bundle at the top, and a brass pot in his left hand. His shoes were torn, but he said he

	was out looking for work. I'd like to go look-ing for things to do, to work maybe.
Madhav:	*⌊softly⌋ Ah! we seek what we cannot find. We find what we do not seek.*
Amal:	*What was that?*
Madhav:	*Nothing. I just wanted to warn you about speaking to strangers.*
Amal:	*But I love to talk to strangers.*
Madhav:	*Someone might take you away, kidnap you.*
Amal:	*That would be so exciting. But no, no one will ever take me away. They all want me*

to stay locked up in here. You and the doctor and everyone else. But the crazy man

was quite harmless. He sat under the fig tree on the river bank and ate his lunch. I told

mother I too would like to get my feet wet and have my lunch on the water's edge.

But she wants me to get well first.

Madhav:	*She's right.*
Amal:	*I know. Well, I guess I'll just sit by this win-dow and think of all the places I could be at this time.*
Madhav:	*But you can't be everywhere at the same time. Well! see you later. I must be off.*

[Exit Madhav]

| Amal: | *I'm sure I could be wherever I wanted to.* |

* * * * *

We stopped, and the wind stopped abruptly. None of us said what was on our minds.

"I must bring the music tomorrow," said Tetsuo, firmly, breaking the silence.

"This looks like a good place to stop," I quickly added, hearing Connie's voice trail away. She was beginning to sound really tired.

We looked up at each other at the same time. Connie and I reached out for our wine glasses. Then we sat in silence as all our thoughts seemed to converge on the play and what meaning it held for Marek. It was all so strange. What could Marek have found in the play that was so interesting? Where was the post office? I felt uneasy and uncomfortable.

"Shall we congratulate ourselves on a fine performance?" I asked. It was a foolish attempt at conversation, for nobody answered. I looked at Connie and saw tears in her eyes. Then I glanced at Tetsuo who had also seen her and decided to remain silent. As our eyes met, I sensed Tetsuo was trying to tell me, "Not me. Perhaps another time, in another place." After a moment's hesitation I pulled Connie into my arms. She dropped her head on my shoulder.

Tetsuo smiled faintly as he got up from the sofa. "Must be going," he said, as he started for the door. Then he stopped and turned round. Looking at Connie, he asked, "Are you sure we can read some more tomorrow night?" Connie nodded her head to say yes.

"You have three more days of freedom, haven't you?" asked Tetsuo. He sounded almost exuberant.

"Yes," I replied.

Tetsuo left us both sitting on the sofa. I still couldn't get over how unreal our voices had seemed. And so I was a bit surprised by Connie's tears. She remained silent. I looked at the wine bottle and the glasses which no one had touched. I poured another glass and offered it to her. She didn't want it. I played with the stem of the glass for a while and emptied it in one gulp.

Connie got up after a while, stretched herself, and held out her hands to me. She was smiling once again.

We bathed once more, very quickly, and slipped into bed. She brought her lips close to my ears and whispered, "Did you have a nice day?"

"I haven't had so much fun any other day," I whispered back. "Thank you," I said as I kissed her on the cheek.

It was easy to fall asleep on a night like this. But I kept wanting to stay awake. "It's strange," I remarked to Connie, "that more people hadn't heard about the book."

"Which one?" she asked.

"Not the play. The other one," I lied.

"Oh!" she laughed softly. "That one. Well, if you follow what it says, it turns the woman into a cross between super-woman and Barbie, and man into a fucking drone. Wouldn't go down well in our society." Long afterwards, before we fell asleep in each others' arms, she sounded reflective. She let out a long sigh and said, "I must be a mare."

I thought about that remark for a moment. A mare? No, certainly not. Whatever magic the book contained, it had transformed her, certainly not into a mare, at least for one afternoon and an evening, and I loved every moment of her magical transformation. It pained me to think we would be separated again by prison walls a few days later. Maybe I would feel like Amal.

꧁꧂

October 12, 1998

Connie left in the early hours of the morning. I didn't sleep well at all in Marek's bed. I think I'll begin this day with another look at Marek's diary. Meanwhile, there's another voice that's dying to speak. Sometimes, I go round in circles, searching for the other voice that starts up in my mind at the oddest moments. Then I have trouble trying to figure out who it is that's speaking. Perhaps there are two voices in my head. It's one or the other that holds court at any time. No sooner have I gotten used to one, then the other tries to take over. This is followed by pangs of uncertainty and doubt as I ask myself, "Whose voice am I listening to?" I have sometimes felt this way while exercising in the prison yard or, earlier, rowing on the river, staring too long at the water, or dreaming of Field, that little town in the Canadian Rockies which, according to Martin Fisher, held a glorious and terrible secret.

Field is more than a place where I grew up. My father's convinced that's where all life came from. It's a nice feeling. What's more, that's where all life returns. He assured me once that's where I'm heading back no matter where I'm going to. It seems I'm headed that way from the very beginning. But he never explained to me what he meant by beginnings. I once had a hunch it had something to do with . . . . with what? The circumstances of my birth? My childhood experiences? The crimes I did or did not commit lately in my youth?

None of these questions have any plausible answers. Not in my mind at least. I think I know better now. And that makes me something of a curiosity for normal people. I interest them because I am something of a freak. I worry about things which rarely concern others. I am obsessed with life and death, with the mysteries of creation. I know it all sounds very odd to people around me.

Half asleep, I saw Connie vaguely when she got up to leave. As I looked at her face, fear of losing her chilled my heart. We had three more days till my time ran out in which to clean out, clear out, the apartment. What then? The thought of violating my brief parole and escaping to Connie's studio apartment keeps crossing my mind. A foolish thought. I couldn't escape even if they let me. I couldn't stay on at Connie's indefinitely, for she too had been talking about going back home. Where was mine? Where could I go? What could I do? Suddenly, it was as if the future held nothing for me. And the past, what use would it be to anyone but me? These thoughts flew in and out of my mind as I walked softly through the apartment, made myself a cup of coffee, and took it across to Marek's writing desk. As I sat there, it amused me to think that Marek's possessions - of questionable value to anyone, despite Connie's enthusiasm - were getting passed on to me. What could I do with them, except store them some place which certainly wouldn't be my own, since I had none.

Now to my homage to Marek for the day. I must carry on with what Matthew unravelled yesterday. Another page from Marek's diary. Can't make out whether it's sad or funny. It's always confusing. Marek had a happy knack of confusing those who asked him questions.

"How did you lose your sight?" I asked him one day.

"I was bedazzled by the glory of God," he said, "much like St. Paul." I recall that he sounded very much like Stan rendering his views on the curious circumstances of my birth.

At the time, St.Paul was lost on me, until I discovered him much later in prison. Marek assured me that a lot of people find religion in prison. There's so little else to find. He did insist though that he had travelled in time and come face to face with the origin of the species, or God, as some people choose to refer to the event. I would have continued to laugh in his face over his unabashed declarations had I not learnt as much about genetics as I did in prison.

Marek would joke with Olga asking her where she got her skill with systems. "Secret German ancestry perhaps," he teased her. "It's all in the genes, you know," he added.

"It was their 'system' that destroyed the Jews," I once heard him tell Tetsuo, when both were in a somewhat reflective mood. "It's not that the Germans were inherently evil. It's simply that they have such a childlike faith in systems. Their system of life and death, their system of God, systems of transportation, music, of order and discipline, reward and retribution. In contrast, the rest of us are so lawless, so disorganized, so given to wanton flights of fancy, predestined victims."

I especially remember that evening's conversation because that was the first time that I heard Marek mention the land formation known as the Devonian Hunsruckschiefer of the Rhine valley, how he felt fascinated by the fossils preserved there for millions of years. It was however my father who happened to explain to me, when the subject accidentally came up sometime during my first months in prison, how Hunsruckschiefer was one of the three great *Lagerstatten*, a "lode place" - much like the Burgess Shale - which hold the secret to the origins of the species. Once this historic affinity had managed to surface, it didn't take long for Marek and Martin Fisher to become soul-mates.

"It was part of my duty, call it my mission, in Treblinka," said Marek, "to help convert human bodies into soft-bodied faunas for what many Germans believed to be the Day of Judgement."

"In what way?" asked my father quietly. I vividly remember the conversation, how my father grew pale and ashen, how he seemed suddenly to age before my eyes.

Marek pointed out that there were three preconditions for the preservation of soft-bodied faunas. First, what was needed was rapid burial in undisturbed sediment. "For this," said Marek, "we simply dug trenches or prepared vast fields of earth." Secondly, the material needed to be buried rapidly in an environment free of the usual agents of immediate destruction, animals and scavengers, for instance. Thirdly, the material had to lie hidden from prying eyes for millions of years. So Marek claimed that he had personally helped melt thousands of bodies which he hoped would remain indistinguishable from plain ordinary earth - hence of little interest to anybody - until the good Lord commanded them to rise someday.

✳ ✳ ✳

TWO

*Maybe I was free of the plague and maybe it was my
friends and neighbours who were to blame. It was they
who had brought this disaster upon us. On the street,
I stopped passers-by, people who knew me and those who
didn't. I stared into their faces, their eyes, to discover
the slightest signs of their terrible scourge. I would grab
hold of their hands, examine the skin under the nails, look
for tell-tale signs on the palms. Oh God! I said to myself,
let me find one fugitive carrier of this disease and then
it shouldn't be difficult to track the others down. Then
those of us who were disease-free could probably go back
to our earlier lives. Coffee and cake and pink mousse at
L'Ourse. I grew more desperate by the day as I realized
I didn't know what the symptoms were I was looking for.
"You're being foolish," Olga told me, "if you're looking
for something and don't know what you're looking for."
Others were less kind. "You're mad," they began to say the
moment they saw me.*

*But I had to keep looking. I felt it was my destiny to set my
people free. It was a lofty thought, but no loftier than those of
Korczak or Czerniakow. I needed to keep searching for those
Jews who were the clandestine carriers of the plague. Bizarre
couplets began to grow in my mind. I started to accost men
and women with them. One of the first ones that I remember:*

> Circumcision is great,
> A simple surgical feat.
> Should they check your foreskin
> In Pawiak prison, you're meat.

They began to press money in my hands to stop me from reciting my verses in the street. I was well and truly in a lunatic world.

> Vayehi erev, vayehi voker.......
> (And there was darkness, and
> there was light, a light filled
> with darkness).

* * *

Voice Two: Misha

Two-One

Matthew lay exhausted from the previous day. Little wonder. So I have to rouse myself. I have no choice. Life must go on.

I am starting to admire Marek afresh. He had a precise sense of where things were in the apartment. After all, he seemed to have gotten by very well without me all this time. My work inside rarely consisted of anything more than bringing things to him - usually some writing that he had been working on - and making sure I put things back in their proper place. His writing material consisted of a flat cardboard box in which he kept three bound note pads, all of the same size. I would observe him going through the motion of feeling his way through each pad until he found what seemed to be the right one for him to write in. Somehow he could always tell where to find a fresh page to write on. One day, I couldn't hide my curiosity any longer. "How can you tell which pad you want?" I asked. He waved me close to the breakfast table on which he worked, took my hand and made me feel the right-hand edge of the black covers where he had little grooves cut into the binding. Each pad had a groove cut into a different spot which stood for a number that he knew. I discovered later it was Olga who had put together the simple system for him. It was easy and I picked it up right away.

Where Marek needed help was in the world outside. He walked rather slowly with a nervous, shuffling gait. The sidewalks were simply too dangerous for him, and his stick didn't help at all. I think he was dying to get out into the open, and that's what we did the first three days that I worked for him. We went walking.

On the third day Marek asked me, for the third evening in a row, to walk him to the glittering blue Sony building at a busy nearby intersection, on the corner of Wladyslawa Andersa and Solidarnosci.

"Are you sure you want to go there again?" I asked, surprised by his request.

Marek stopped on the doorway to his apartment, lifted up the slate hanging from a piece of string round his neck, and wrote quickly: "Must."

"Sure," I said.

I led him out through the door and he handed me his apartment keys, three large keys and several smaller ones in a worn leather pouch. The leather was cracking and as soon as I tried it I realized the zipper didn't work. I struggled with it for a few minutes until the entire zipper, all six inches of it, parted company with the pouch. Although there were three large door keys, he had instructed me on the first evening to use only two. I used the first to turn the main lock on the door, then I used the other to put the deadbolt in place. Once he had his hand on the stairwell banister, Marek moved quite quickly, without any help from me.

Outside, I held his hand and carefully crossed the street to avoid an enormous construction rig that blocked the sidewalk. "There are some brand new apartments coming up here," I said. "Maybe you could move into one that was bright and sunny."

He nodded his head as if to say it wasn't for him. A sad smile played around his lips.

The wind was cool and I stopped to pull my scarf tightly round my neck. Standing there with a blank expression on his face, Marek looked sad like the old statues I passed on my way, statues which hadn't been cleaned for ages. For the first time, I felt sorry for him. I fixed his scarf as well, then buttoned the two top buttons of his overcoat. As I was finishing with the last button, he raised his hand and touched mine. I saw a flicker of a smile on Marek's face.

I must've been in love with Olga, that's probably why my thoughts keep coming back to her. When you're like me, it seems more natural to fall in love with older women. I just don't know why. The first time I saw her, it was a cold winter's evening, nothing like the previous night. I was just starting to become familiar with the neighbourhood. The soft evening light made the houses look less dilapidated than they had first appeared to me in the bright daylight. Marek and I had just about turned the corner when a silver-haired woman came to a halt directly in front of us. I imagined she would be in her seventies, about the same age as Marek.

"Oh!" she gasped, putting her hand on my shoulder. "Oh!" she said again. "I can't believe it. You look like a nice young man. What's your name?" she asked.

"Misha," I believe I told her.

"Listen to me, Misha," she said. "Don't let this old man fill your head with rubbish. He may be blind and pretends to be dumb sometimes, but he can still write the most awful things on that slate of his. What's worse, he can hear everything we say." With that she burst out laughing.

"You're mocking me again, Olga," the old man suddenly blurted out. After a moment's pause, he joined in the laughter too, but stopped abruptly. I was amazed. So he could speak, after all. From that moment onwards, Marek rarely used the slate to communicate when he was in my company.

"It's a voice I save only for the ones I love," said Marek. "My silence protects me like a wall from the contempt of others."

"I'm Olga," she said, introducing herself. "You'll look after him, Misha, won't you?" she asked, uttering my name with a sweetness even my mother was never capable of. With that, she lifted up my cap, kissed me on my forehead, and gently placed the cap back on my head.

So that was the evening I met Olga for the first time, when I discovered that Marek could speak if he chose to. I felt good that he had decided not to inflict the slate on me any longer. Matthew was a little surprised, and pleased as well. I was delighted.

One day, feeling and looking a little depressed for some reason, Marek confessed that he pretended to be dumb not only to attract pity but to over-state his helplessness. That evening was the closest we had come to the building. "What's this?" asked Marek, tapping lightly on the glass with his cane.

"It's the glass wall of this huge building we're standing in front of," I replied.

"No," said Marek, making a face. "These days you young fellows can't see a thing. It's the Synagogue on Tlomackie."

"There's no synagogue here. It's all blue glass."

"Ha! Blue did you say?"

"Yes," I replied.

"How high?"

"Oh! Five hundred feet maybe."

"How wide?"

I was naturally reduced to guessing at this point. "Three hundred," I suggested.

Marek furrowed his brow in deep concentration. "I think I know what's happened," he said, still wrapped in thought.

Just then, an Oriental gentleman in a spotless white shirt with a bright red tie stepped out of one of the main entrance to the building which was slightly to the right of us. "Excuse me," he said politely, bowing slightly to Marek. "This is the third evening in a row that I've sat in the coffee bar on the other side of this glass and seen you. Both of you," he said, moving his glance to me. "I'm curious. Can I be of any help?"

"No, no, I've found the answer." Marek shook his head adamantly as he started to wheel around to leave.

The gentleman, whose racial identity I had by this time narrowed down to either Chinese or Japanese, smiled and bowed once more. "I'm Tetsuo Hashimoto. Won't you please come with me to my office and I will order some coffee and pastries from the cafe downstairs. I'm so curious." I was amused to see the gentleman bow repeatedly in the direction of a blind man. Surely, he knew by now Marek couldn't see a thing.

I looked at Marek's face for an answer. He smiled, turned slightly, and allowed me to lead him into the building. Following the stranger, our host, we entered through a glass entrance door into a large, glittering elevator panelled with mirrors. I had seen such elevators before, but I think Matthew was full of wonder. I worried to think that Marek, once our host engaged him in conversation, would perhaps revert to the slate.

"Only other building like this I've seen is the Marriott. I hated it. Still do," whispered Matthew in my ears.

"I think the man is Japanese," I whispered back. "He looks too smart to be Chinese."

The elevator stopped a couple of times on the lower floors to let out a few people. Then it sped upwards, silently, as I stared at the elevator panel. My eyes briefly caught sight of the look of alarm on Marek's face, even as his eyes remained quite expressionless. He appeared more relaxed once we stopped at our destination and I led him out to a vast space on what must have been the topmost floor of the building. We walked straight into a dazzling suite of offices the likes of which neither Matthew nor I had ever seen before. There were several women who, by the blank faces they turned towards us, I assumed to be working for Tetsuo. At the far corner of the room, listening intently to music that suddenly greeted our ears, was a young woman who at least flashed a welcoming smile at us. This was obviously Tetsuo's office, and the pretty woman in a fashionable black dress didn't look like no secretary. Tetsuo introduced her to us as Connie Taylor. Even as we shook hands, I think Matthew fell a little in love with Connie right away. Perhaps it was natural that it be Matthew who succumbed, for he seemed hopelessly drawn towards smart, intelligent women.

"I've heard that music before," said Marek. I breathed a sigh of relief at hearing Marek speak. But I could sense he was very excited.

"But that's impossible." Tetsuo stopped in his tracks, looking a little agitated. "The music's been recorded only six months ago. It's not been released in the market yet."

Marek's brows remained wrinkled. There was an expression of intense concentration on his face.

"Where do you suppose you might've heard it?" asked Connie, glancing quickly from Tetsuo to Marek.

"I heard it as Misha and I stood in front of your building, looking in. I've been hearing it for years, nearly fifty years."

Tetsuo exchanged glances with Connie and shrugged his shoulders. Our tea and cakes had followed us without Tetsuo having shouted any instructions to anyone. Connie poured some tea for us and handed Marek his cup. Matthew and I wasted no time in tackling the cakes. "Do you know," asked Marek, "that this building should never have been here? This is where stood the great Warsaw Synagogue, blown up under orders from a despicable man, Stroop. This building too should be torn down."

Tetsuo laughed light-heartedly. "Look Mr. Rubinstein," he said, "we're in the business of communication, not of preserving old buildings or their memory." Later, I would demand from Tetsuo an explanation for the word, communication. What was this communication, since I always thought the company made CD's and Walkmans.

Marek smiled, finished the cake he was eating, and returned his cup to the table. "You can't destroy the memory for me," he said. "I'm unimportant. It's the others I'm thinking about. Others who never saw the Jewish synagogue on Tlomackie."

"What was it like?" asked Connie.

"It was the most beautiful building I have ever known. Some said its dome was like that of the Paris Opera. But I don't think it looked anything like a church or an exotic eastern building. It looked every inch a secular building. We tried so hard to deserve the love of others, we imitated, copied, borrowed. The porch and dome of the facade even looked like the Pantheon in Rome."

Tetsuo couldn't resist another comment. "And that," he asked, "in spite of the Romans destroying the Temple of Jerusalem?"

"Yes, I'm afraid so," replied Marek, "but the choir will sing no more, nor will the organ shake the dome and send shivers through the congregation." Marek paused to wipe his tears. While we sat and listened in silence, he told us how it cost three hundred thousand rubles, one hundred and twenty years ago, to build the synagogue. A few wealthy Jews contributed the money needed, as well as one kind Catholic who sent fifty rubles for the building, and fifty more for the poor.

"Maybe the Catholics wanted their money back," joked Tetsuo.

"With interest that would put the meanest Shylock to shame," suggested Connie.

I sat in silence, ignoring the remaining cakes laid out in front of us. Crystal Night, Rabbi Poznanski, St. Charles Borromeo, and the Pantheon - the names were magical and showed up my ignorance. *Adair, Adair*, whispered Matthew and promised me that he would never forget, not a single name, not a single word, not a single face.

"It has taken you two thousand years to figure out why God allowed the destruction of the Temple in Jerusalem," said Tetsuo. "Now you'll argue for the next two thousand years why Jews allowed six million of their own to be murdered by the Germans."

"But that is not true," I protested. It was my turn to describe the books Mr. Kerrigan brought to class and held aloft as Jewish propaganda. I remembered that several of them had pictures of large groups of naked women, some with children in their arms. They were supposed to be pictures of women about to be gassed to death in Treblinka. I remembered the name because it was one of the only places I associated with Warsaw when we decided to move. Mr. Kerrigan even gave us a large magnifying glass and asked us to see for ourselves. "Look at their faces," he said, "the women are actually smiling. You believe they are going to die? For all you know, it's a picture of women getting into the baths somewhere, like the hot springs in some resort or the other."

I stopped as I caught sight of Tetsuo staring at me. Marek sat with tears staining his cheeks, but there was now a smile on his face. He reached out and gently placed his hand on my arm. "I will tell you about Treblinka," he said.

Tetsuo cleared his throat and looked me straight in the eye. "Young man," he said, "have you heard of Hiroshima?" I nodded my head and pleaded ignorance. "That's one of two Japanese cities where America dropped the atom bomb." I said I knew about the atom bomb. Then Tetsuo grew thoughtful and asked if I knew why the bomb had been dropped on Japan. For some reason, my thoughts had returned to Mr. Kerrigan and the pictures of the Treblinka women, and I felt myself answering in a dream.

But it was Matthew who found his voice first. "Could it be something to do with genes?" he asked.

A long silence followed. "You find out," said Tetsuo. "I don't really know." He looked around his ordered, glass-walled office, then fixed his gaze in the distance, to the fading mosaic of leafless trees which stood over the snow-covered park where, as he later told me, only a few hours earlier, he had enjoyed a pleasant lunch-hour break with Connie, the American record company executive, and watched her with mounting excitement as she tossed pieces of her sandwich to the hundreds of ducks, fat and bored, who had waddled and converged upon their park-bench from every direction. Matthew and I had seen the scenario played out so many times that we had no reason to believe it might have been otherwise than as described by Tetsuo. A day would come when Matthew too would share lunch with Connie in the park. "Strrroop," said Tetsuo, lingering over the 'r'. He paused and continued to look into the distance. "Strrrrooop," he repeated, rolling the 'r' over his tongue even longer this time. "What do I care for Strroop?" he asked, turning abruptly to face Marek. "Damn Stroop."

"Yes, thank you," nodded Marek. "They hanged him in this very city forty five years ago."

The stars were out that evening as I walked home after seeing Marek to his apartment. I pictured the Warsaw synagogue in the sky and saw its Corinthian columns etched in white. I saw the galleried nave, exactly as Marek had described it, crowded with stars, and a milky whiteness shimmering between the stars which I thought to be the sacred scroll. And the stars themselves, could it be that they were the six million murdered Jews that Tetsuo was talking about? But then, what about Mr. Kerrigan, for whom the genes were the immortals. Could it be that the stars were the genes, let loose from their magic bottles?

Two-Two

Everyone wanted to teach us something. Marek wanted to tell me about Treblinka. Lydia wanted to teach me how to make love. And Tetsuo wanted to teach me about war. "War is something like the emperor's new clothes," he said. I could relate to it right away, but even more by the time he had finished his story. "Once there was a great emperor," said Tetsuo, "and all he wanted to do was spend time with his many lovers." I of course could see nothing wrong with that, for I hated violence myself.

"The last thing on his mind was war," Tetsuo continued. "But his subjects wanted entertainment, vast spectacles, and the emperor's romances, however interesting, were getting tedious. In fact, there were pockets of intrigue beginning to surround his love life, women becoming vengeful when they fell out of his favour, courtiers secretly plotting to overthrow him. So the emperor decided to go to war against a far away tyrant who had a pet dragon that was ravaging the surrounding kingdoms. His subjects loved the idea of war; it was so much more dramatic than his boring palace romances.

"Each day the king put on a new suit of shining armour, however reluctantly, and rode a white horse in the market place to show his warlike intent, even as his soldiers were closing in on the distant kingdom. After a few days of this show on the horse the king started to love the warm adulation from his subjects. Things couldn't be going better for him. He continued to have all the women he wanted without drawing attention away from the exciting prospect of his generals and soldiers slaying the tyrant and his dragon.

"It was summertime, the days were getting warmer, and the soldiers hadn't returned home. One morning the king left his bed, climbed his horse, and headed for the marketplace for his daily spectacle. Only, on this warm morning he had overlooked the armour. In fact, this morning he wore no clothes. Some people were startled at first. But others saw the emperor's bronzed young body and thought he looked like one of the Greek warriors whose statues you see in museums. In the eyes of these loyal folk, the emperor couldn't have chosen a better suit of armour.

"The people got used to seeing their king in the nude, riding his white stallion in the marketplace. About this time some deserters from his army began to return to the city. At first, the local people showered scorn on these stragglers. But they pleaded they were not cowards. Finally, they made a startling revelation. There was no dragon in the tyrant's kingdom. They saw no need to leave their families and chase chimeras in distant lands.

"One of the deserters was a young boy who started to mingle with the crowds who watched the king ride by each morning. As he watched one morning, the emperor - by now, quite bored with his daily ritual - began to daydream. And a strange spectacle reared up before the people's eyes. The king started to have an erection. His cock grew and grew like a balloon, except that it was pumped up with his warm blood, not air. Gigantic, it even put the horse to shame.

"There's our monster, our dragon," screamed the young boy, pointing to the emperor's cock. Other deserters in the crowd looked up and picked up the cry. In a flash, all these men were rushing towards the king. They surrounded the horse, dragged the king off its back, and hacked off his cock.

They danced all morning with the cock stuck on a spear, intoxicated with their new-found victory. But when they sat down, exhausted, they saw that the cock was no larger than yours or mine, which was a real downer for everyone.

"So is war," said Tetsuo, with a shrug, as he wrapped up his story.

Marek was listening with his head drooping over his chest. He now lifted his up his face, smiled, but said nothing.

"You must have stories to tell, old man," said Tetsuo, turning to Marek. "Tell them to me, and I will meld to your words the music you love so much, the music that has been blowing through your mind these past fifty years. I will erect a monument to man's inhumanity to man. I once lived by the sea in a place called Minamata, went fishing, ate oranges and persimmons fresh off the branches. Listened to the wind's lullabies. Now it's all gone, much like your synagogue, destroyed by human hands."

Marek said nothing.

In the weeks that followed, we developed quite a friendship, Tetsuo, Marek, Connie, and I. "Too bad you're not a pianist," said Tetsuo to Marek, "or we would've made a recording artist out of you." I very nearly blurted out that Marek was writing a song, but stopped myself at the last moment. Connie was real cute, and Matthew would look at her and wonder if she was having sex with Tetsuo. I couldn't think why else she would be staying on in Warsaw, because she said herself that she liked her work with the American company even though it was much smaller than Tetsuo's.

Lydia had grown more solemn over the past few weeks and that pained me a lot because I wanted her to look happy, to smile as she kissed me goodbye in the morning. Besides, she was my mother, wasn't she? I would look at Connie's pretty face, almost always smiling, and wish I could transfer the smile to Lydia's.

One evening, Tetsuo asked me for dinner at a neat little restaurant in town. I couldn't wait to mention it to Stan; instead, I merely told Matthew. Connie was also there. I think I must have drunk my glass of wine rather quickly, for I suddenly felt bolder and my head lighter. Matthew's curiosity kept urging me on, and I finally asked Tetsuo what Connie was doing in Warsaw. He replied that she was trying to steal some Polish composers away from his company, and he thought she would have some success. But the real reason, he said, leaning over and patting Connie's tummy, was that she was going to have his baby. I do not why, but I felt very happy, not only for Connie, but Tetsuo as well.

Two-Three

Lydia and I became so close that soon I knew every nook and cranny in her body. But I might as well have been as blind as Marek, for I never saw her naked from a distance until the night it still pains me to think about. "Didn't you ever have a baby?" I asked her that night. And she started to laugh. In the pale street light that seemed always to lift one corner of the curtain and creep into our room, she looked at me with surprise and amusement and said, "You know all about babies, don't you?"

"Oh yeah," I replied, trying to sound wise and grown-up.

Lydia remained silent for a long time, then said, "They took me to a hospital when I was five and when I came back home my mother was crying. I felt all right but she told me I would never have babies because of what they had done to me in the hospital. I found out much later that whatever was done to me was because I was called a Rhineland bastard." I wonder if I remember Rhineland as the name of a place or as a name for Lydia! What her mother said to her didn't make sense to her at the time because Lydia had a mother and a father. So why call her a bastard? When she was old enough to really want a baby herself, she found out that there was a time when having a mother and a father wasn't enough. Her father had to be a German just like her mother, which he wasn't. He was Algerian.

That was when she told me about Misha, the child she could only have in her imagination. I felt sad thinking there might be a whole world of children of the imagination out there somewhere, children who never came to life, or came to life all too briefly. Wouldn't it be strange, I thought, to come

73

face to face with Misha, or Olga's little daughter - whose story is the saddest of all - when one day I ceased to be as real as Matthew and became, like Olga and Marek, figures that were impossible to make out between creations of the imagination and real figures that popped up in memory from time to time.

There came a period when Martin Fisher was gone for a really long time. He would of course phone every so often, but he failed to show up. Lydia began to look distracted and I wondered if she was short of money. Then she started coming home in the evenings with strange men. This drove me nuts because it meant I had to sleep in my own room. But of course I lay awake practically all night, listening to their laughter, the sound of bare backs and buttocks being slapped, and Lydia's moans. After three or four months of this, I decided to give her up. What helped me make up my mind was the night I woke up from a terrible nightmare in which I found myself running, running, running. First, I was running through a wet forest crawling with insects, thick shrubs and tendrils. Then I found myself in a narrow street through which was hurtling all kinds of furniture like in a *Star Wars* movie. I had to duck and twist to avoid being hit by tables, chairs, dressers, flower pots until I could run no more. My path was blocked by a pile of debris, furniture of all kinds heaped together. Suddenly, out of nowhere, my father shows up with a lighted torch in one hand. He sets fire to all the stuff that's piled high like a bonfire and, whoosh, the whole place goes up in flames. Then he throws the burning torch at me. I screamed in terror, and ran straight for Lydia's bed.

The light was on in her room. There she was, all naked and shiny, sitting on top of Mr. Mansell, gently rocking to and fro, making love to him. I will never forget the look on her face as I bounded through the door and stood in front of her. There was something amazing about her which I had never noticed before. It never occurred to me that an ageing body could be so supple and graceful, so removed from the awkwardness and imperfections of youth. She was like nature - forests, winding rivers, snow-clad peaks seen through a window, from a distance. You see nothing but the lines of a ridge or the curves of a valley and everything looks so perfect. She looked so beautiful I almost felt ashamed to have become an intruder. I didn't run away from her, simply turned and walked slowly back to my room.

To this day, I am haunted by that beautiful sight, that curved body that branched out like a tree from the limp earth of Mr. Mansell's flesh. And I wondered how strange it is that people should make love hidden from other eyes. I have read somewhere that primitive tribes had no inhibitions about engaging in sex in public. In groups, I suppose. I must have seen at least two dozen different men go through Lydia's room the past few months. Would it be any less exciting, I thought, if all the men gathered in the same room with Lydia, and their wives and their girl-friends and other casual one-night stands and kept grunting and moaning and gasping until exhausted? But I suppose that while our laws do not prevent us from engaging in group sex in some form or the other, we must resort to individual sorties as a matter of convenience and caution.

To say that I, Misha, was disillusioned is to put it mildly. That's when I made up my mind to leave Lydia to others. From that day, she was little more than a mother to me, and she was a good mother, mind you. But I found it difficult to forgive Mr. Mansell for whom I had felt some friendship, thanks perhaps to the gifts he brought me from time to time. But what had he done for Lydia? I really felt she deserved better than what she got.

As Martin Fisher's visits to Warsaw became more and more infrequent, a succession of strangers continued to pass through our apartment and Lydia's life. Mr. Mansell flew in dutifully from Boston every month and continued to visit the apartment for a few days at a time. I kept my distance and avoided him.

Just as I never forgot Lydia's beautiful body, I never forgave Mr. Mansell either. He tried to make up to me afterwards, bringing me Godiva chocolates instead of crummy Mars bars. But I could never eat them, and ended up sharing them between Lydia and my friends. One day, when Lydia was late coming home in the evening, Mr. Mansell buzzed the apartment and walked in, reeking of alcohol and garlic. He seemed a little annoyed that Lydia wasn't there to pour him the drink that I knew he wanted. Finally, he asked me if I would bring him a glass and the bottle of scotch. If I had felt differently about him, I would've offered to get out some ice cubes and pour him his drink, but I didn't. "Sit down," he said, after I had placed the bottle and glass on the table in front of him.

"Don't you miss your dad sometimes?" he asked.

"Sometimes."

He gulped a mouthful of his drink, closing his eyes as he tilted his head back. "You haven't told him about Lydia and me, have you?"

"It's none of my business, Mr. Mansell," I replied.

"That's my boy," he said, putting his hand on my shoulder and drawing me closer. "Grown-ups must learn to keep secrets."

I nodded, trying not to be overpowered by his garlic smell which seized me inside my nostrils and my throat. Suddenly, he moved his right hand in a flash and unzipped his trousers. Another deft movement, and Mr. Mansell's enormous cock leapt out of his underwear. I felt transfixed by the sight, a glistening pink stump glaring out of his black pin-striped Brooks Brothers pants. I remembered the name Brooks Brothers because Mr. Mansell always prided himself on his clothes and the name never failed to raise the dumb question in my mind: I wonder what the Brooks Sisters do? Blindly, I let him guide my hand to this object of his. There was a pleading look in Mr. Mansell's eyes, which seemed quite at odds with the flaming sword he was about to place in my hand. Adair, Adair, I whispered in my terror. But my fingers touched something metallic instead, and I thought it very strange because one doesn't normally expect to strike metal in those parts of a man's body. I looked closely and realized that my fingers had stumbled upon the shiny brass zippers that Mr. Mansell had undone so effortlessly only moments ago. It almost looked like gold, and I thought maybe the famous Brooks Brothers treated their rich customers to gold zippers.

I have always had this strange thing about zippers. Not anything vicious, mind you, even though I half destroyed Mr. Rubenstein's key pouch. When I look at zippers, they look back at me. Some smile, others look sad - I'm talking about short zippers, the six-inch kind. The longer ones I find rather nondescript, quite characterless. I tend to leave them alone. Mr. Mansell's was the smiling kind. A strange thrill shot through me as my thumb and forefinger latched onto the tongue. Zipp. Pull. Zip. I managed to zip up the fly just as smoothly as Mr. Mansell had zipped it open. Almost immediately, Mr. Mansell let out an ungodly scream. I think the brass zipper had somehow zipped his trousers onto his cock. Once more, I was filled with terror - but also a sense of amusement - at the sight of the blood, suddenly blooming like an enormous flower, darkening his trousers and his white Brooks Brothers shirt. I wondered if the Brooks Sisters helped their brothers by washing their customers' clothes. Desperate and confused, I tried to unzip again. To my horror, Mr. Mansell let out an even more blood-curdling scream. For some reason, the zipper had lost its earlier smoothness. It refused to budge. I think if it had been gold, it wouldn't have been any problem. But what do you expect with brass? Eventually, I had to call an ambulance to send Mr. Mansell to the hospital. What happened there I cannot tell, because when I saw Mr. Mansell again we were in no mood for pleasantries.

The neighbours came out see what was happening. Many of them knew Mr. Mansell from his earlier visits, but he just kept moaning as the paramedics helped him out the door; he did not answer any of their questions. As a grown-up, I felt obliged to keep Mr. Mansell's secret, and brushed off all questions by whining incoherently to show how upset I was and shaking my head. But when Lydia came home, I had to ask her if, as a grown-up herself, she could keep a secret if I shared it with her. She said she would and I described to her what had happened. Then I helped her clean the bloodstains from the sofa and she drew me into her arms and said she always thought buttons were better than zippers. And the old laughter returned to her.

Two-Four

But for what happened one pleasant, lazy and silent after-noon about five years ago, I might never have seen the inside of a prison. On that afternoon, Stan and I sat on a low wall not far from Krasinski's Garden and licked our ice-creams. On other days, the storekeepers would have chased us away, but not today.

"Sundays are so boring," declared Stan, as he kicked the wall with the back of his dangling feet. There was a loud thud as the bottom of his roller blades crashed against a metal sign advertising some business or the other. The sound was like a signal that goaded him on. Stan just kept on banging rhyth-mically with his feet without a break.

There was nobody on the street in front of us. The near-est people were a couple of hundred yards away where some stalls had laid out their merchandise - dolls, cardigans, min-iature chess boards, dried fruits, flowers - in the hope of sales to tourists. I found the sound tedious and irritating after a while. "Do you mind stopping it?" I finally asked.

"Shut up. I'll do what I want."

I said nothing, and turned my attention instead to breaking off small pieces of the cone now that the ice-cream was level with its edges. I guess it was the Gypsy in him that made him appear so eccentric, so tormented from time to time. Still, if he continued with his perverse mood much longer I decided I would leave and pay Marek a visit. Marek was just around the corner, only a couple of minutes away on my blades. I kept nibbling away at the wafer. Stan decided that he had had enough and chucked his cone onto the street. The wafer cone didn't smash and the little ice-cream left inside it didn't spill over on the cobblestones. The cone rolled from one side to the other and came to a stop. Stan nimbly jumped off the wall and slid over to it. I thought he was going to squish it onto the stones with his blades. Instead, he reached into his pocket and brought out a metal hammer. It was not too large, but it wasn't very small either. I asked him what he did with the hammer. He didn't answer, just made a face and shrugged his shoulders. Then he squatted down and proceeded to flatten the cone against the stones with his hammer. Soon there was a light brown triangle on the dark stone with some melted ice-cream staining the surface around it. Stan stood up and, fixing his gaze on the spot, turned his head from side to side as if admiring a work of art.

I was glad the banging had stopped, but I felt a strange unease. The fun seemed to have gone out of each other's company. On other afternoons earlier that summer, we would sit near the Martyr's Memorial and watch buses unload visitors from foreign lands. We played a game trying to guess where they were from. Then we would walk up to them together and ask them questions like: "America?", "Japan?", or "Spain?" Usually, they would smile and reply "Japan, yes," or "No, Canada," or simply "Spain," and Stan and I would look at each other in acknowledgement of who had won and who lost.

The game seemed harmless enough through the summer weekends until summer drew to a close and the number of buses grew less and less, or the buses simply did not come while we hung around. Afterwards, we rollerbladed a lot, but the streets weren't so good and I didn't much care for it.

That particular afternoon, we had gotten tired of waiting near the Martyrs' Memorial for some of Stan's buddies. So we moved along. A solitary person walking the street towards us now caught my attention. The strong sun cast dark shadows on the sidewalk and made it difficult to see very far. All I could make out was that the woman was carrying a bunch of flowers in her hand. I didn't pay any further attention to her until I heard her stop about ten feet away and a familiar voice say, "Bless my soul, I wouldn't have expected to find you here."

"Olga," I cried, as I jumped up on my feet with a clattering sound. I was surprised to see her too even though she didn't live far away. "I didn't think you bought your flowers from those thieves," I said, pointing to the stalls in the distance.

"Ah! today is special. I wanted to surprise Marek because he has finished writing his play, or whatever it is he was writing, the one that'll make him famous."

"Have you read it?"

"Oh, heavens, no. But he says he has a role for me, that of a flower girl." Olga burst out laughing. "A pretty old flower girl."

"You're not old, Olga," I said, teasing her. "You look just like a little girl. Doesn't she?" I asked, turning to Stan.

I noticed for a brief moment that Stan didn't answer. He was still looking at his work of art. Olga broke the silence. "I wish I was a little girl," she said wistfully.

"You know, Stan, don't you?" I asked. "He's too busy admiring his latest work of art." Olga nodded her head. "Do you think Marek will let us hear the play?" I asked, remembering how confused I was with his first reference to the poem and the poet who had inspired him. Tagore or not Tagore! The name always conjured images of matadors and angry bulls.

"Marek has so much going on," sighed Olga. "His plays, his dreams, it's difficult to keep track of him."

I didn't realize Stan had heard me. He waited for Olga to finish, then whirled around unexpectedly, faced us, and said with a sneer and a snarl, "I have other art on my mind."

Startled, both Olga and I remained silent, Afterwards, we walked a little, and found a bench where Olga said it felt good to sit down for a while. Stan kept hovering in the distance. I dusted the leaves off the bench with my hands. We sat down and breathed the somewhat damp autumn smells of fragrant flowers that were all but gone. Olga asked me what I had been up to, as we hadn't run into each other in Marek's apartment for some time. I told her about school, it was quite boring. About my friends, they were okay.

There was a lightness, and also something that grown-ups call dignity, about Olga that I never found in anyone her age or younger. What I grew to feel for Olga was a kind of love I had never felt for anyone else. That is, if it is possible for a thirteen year old to fall in love with someone who was nearing seventy. How am I to know? Sometimes, when I visited Marek in the evenings, she would be there. Olga would let me in, then go and sit with him by the window. In the twilight, the room would be dark and I never thought of switching on the lights. Instead, if there was nothing else to do, I would go and sit beside Olga, and she would take my hand in hers as well. Often, we would listen to music for hours until it was time for me to go home.

They were such magical moments. We didn't speak much. We didn't need to. I would feel myself lulled into a half-sleep from which I would suddenly awaken hearing the sound of a police siren or the screeching wheels of a tramcar making a turn at one of the nearby intersections of Stawki and Jana Pawla. Afterwards, she would fuss around putting together a small supper for us. A bowl of soup and some bread maybe, some cheese and crackers, and her special cookies and cakes that I craved for, especially since Lydia didn't seem that interested in baking for me at home any more.

I often wondered what Olga and Marek spoke to each other when I wasn't around. Tranquil, that's the word. How could they look so tranquil? When we held hands and sat quietly in the darkness I was drawn close to Marek as well. Which seems rather odd because at other times there wasn't the same feeling between us. There was a warm feeling of peace that spread through the three of us, completely engulfing us. Marek once wrote something on a piece of paper which he gave to me when Olga wasn't there. It read: "There are jewel boxes in both our hearts and what we treasure in them are jewels of pain - radiant, crystalline, with a thousand dazzling faces. Olga measures her pain through laughter." I still have the scrap of paper among my things although I had no idea then what he was talking about. But Marek also said he wished he could hear the music once again, the music I at least had heard for the first time in Tetsuo's office somewhere in the clouds. This I could understand, because I would've liked to hear the music too, and it hadn't yet started to switch itself on and off in my mind without my wanting it to as it would very soon.

Usually, we would leave together if Olga happened to be visiting in the evening. At her doorstep, before I went off to catch a tram, she would always plant a kiss on my forehead, moving aside my Bluejays baseball cap as always.

"How I wish I was a little girl," Olga sighed again.

And I remembered it all. How I was walking Olga home one night, and I said I was not in a hurry to get home and she said she would stand me coffee in a rather dimly lit place on the corner. We sat in silence for a long time, and then she said, "I too had a little girl once."

I stared at her face for a long time, wanting her to go on. Then I left my chair to sit next to her on her seat against the wall. And she continued. "I can talk about it now and there are no tears. She was such a happy child. Whenever she met one of her friends she would embrace them or clasp their hands and dance in circles, jumping up and down with joy. It was on her fourth birthday that the Germans burst into our apartment and asked her father, very politely, to step outside. We had just finished supper and hadn't even put out the two candles we had lit to celebrate the occasion. Then we heard a single shot and David was lying in a pool of blood, staring at me in disbelief, dead. Many a night I lay awake wondering what would've happened if I had walked out with David, as I had wanted to at the time. Instead, I sat cowering in the room, clutching Rebecca to my heart. And that was the way it was when the Germans came looking for us some days later, to chase us out into the street and then march us to the *Umschlagplatz*. Rebecca was ill and crying all evening. In our hiding place in the attic I pressed her to my breast so the Germans searching the apartment wouldn't hear her cry. All the time she had her hands, burning with fever, encircling my neck. When the Germans had gone, she too had gone. I must have suffocated my lovely baby. And I have lived on, when there was no reason to."

I remembered how I turned my head and snuggled close to her. And I cried, but Olga didn't.

"Well," she said, "I must put these flowers in the sink before I take them to Marek this evening. You'll come too, won't you?"

"Of course, I will."

"Good bye," she said. "Good bye, Stan."

Then the unexpected happened. Stan whirled around on his blades and struck a tremendous blow with the hammer on Olga's left temple. I rushed to her as she fell. Stan struck again and again and again. I held Olga's head in my arm until Stan pushed me aside viciously and I fell on my back.

Stan stood back, both hands on his hips, and smiled. "Now there's a work of art," he said. "A dead Jew."

I scrambled off the ground and my first instinct was to run for help. This I did, muttering *Adair, Adair* under my breath all the time. I speeded away from Stan and Olga not knowing where I was going. Then, suddenly I knew where I was headed for. To Marek's. I unhooked my blades and ran up the stairs, past another resident who happened to be walking in. I banged on the door, but there was no answer. Where could he be? Wherever, he couldn't have gone very far. Perhaps another tenant might have taken him shopping or for a breath of fresh air. I found him not far away, sitting on the steps to a jewelry store. I dragged Marek down the steps to where Olga lay. She was lying on the ground when we arrived. A crowd of a dozen or so had gathered. They stood some distance away, uncertain, somewhat fearful, perhaps stunned. And Marek held Olga in his arms for the last time.

Two-Five

They were the dearest of friends, Marek and Olga, even though they lived apart from each other - one or two blocks away, depending on whether you walked left or right as you came out of his apartment. I kept asking myself what I could've done to save her, but there were no answers. I kept going over and over the motions in my mind. First it was a blow on the left side, then the right side of her head, then she closed her eyes and moaned for a while and fell silent. I cradled her head for a moment as she fell, until I too was pushed away. Yes, I think I know how I got this disease, even though I was like a sleep-walker the day I suspect my infection first started. I was certainly in a daze when I found myself in front of Marek's building. I was still shivering later when I led Marek back up the dark staircase and entered his place. I started to tell him my story while the old man listened impassively, never even twitching a muscle in his face. Then he let out a howl like a wounded dog, and it continued until it seemed there was no longer any sound left in his body. He paused long enough to catch his breath and then cried out, "For Jews the Day of Yahweh has come and gone. For fifty years I have waited for His sword to slice into the heart of our oppressors. But it hasn't."

I had never seen Marek in such a state before. I was torn between trying to make sense of his grief and wanting to see how an old man could accept tragedy without flinching. It felt horribly warm and stuffy inside the apartment. I sat cowering in front of him, trying to make myself appear small, willing myself to shrink into invisibility. He grew wilder every moment. Now he would sit up in his chair, the next instant he was restlessly pacing the floor, stumbling over the edges of rugs, bumping into chairs and tables that cluttered his little apartment. I was too fearful to pay attention to his endless babble, except that he always kept coming back to the question. Why? He cried, he sobbed, he struck his forehead with his fists, but every outburst ended with the question. Why?

I forced myself briefly to echo the same question. Why, indeed? But I had neither the old man's passion nor his persistence. I was too distractible, my mind soon turned to other things like street sounds. There were people on the street. They seemed unaffected by unexpected tragedies, or were they? Why? They seemed oblivious to sadness, or were they? Why? A street-car rattled and screeched in the distance as it turned a corner. Was it drawing nearer or moving away from us? The wailing siren of an ambulance echoed mournfully in the twilight. Would it reach its destination in time, or was it too late? Why? I found these questions as compelling as Marek's "Why?".

Still, I was a little afraid. Not of Marek, not of any consequences. Perhaps a tinge of remorse over what I had been a part of. I was more bewildered than fearful, more confused than penitent. Marek made matters worse by switching on the stereo. I was so wrapped up in my own thoughts that I hadn't noticed when he had stopped pacing to select a tape, nor when he had pushed it into his tape-deck. *Jesu, Joy of Man's Desiring* suddenly flooded the room with the sound of what seemed like a hundred strings. Now the old man stood still, staring at the two black, squat and ugly speakers resting on the stained marble mantelpiece, tears streaming down his face.

I had often caught Marek listening to the song, sitting next to Olga, holding her hand tightly in his. They would listen to the song mostly in the evenings, with the apartment in darkness and only the tired light of the dying sun filtering through the windows, much like that evening. In the course of the few months I had worked for him I must have heard the song on fifty different occasions at least. I never disturbed them while the music played. But I was witness to something very strange. Every time the song ended, he would look plaintively at Olga and ask, "How could such beautiful music ever come from such cruel people?" The old woman, her eyes bright and shining with pleasure the song held for her, never said a word. She simply shook her head in what seemed a sense of disbelief every time.

I remember Olga as if it was yesterday. Will I ever forget? But strange things happen when two faces fight for focus and attention in the mind. In the present case, both faces belonged to Olga. One face was the smiling, cheerful face I had always known. The other . . . . . The wailing ambulance returned, spoiling the music somewhat. Marek made a face and walked away from the mantelpiece which framed a fireplace where I had never seen a fire, only pieces of crumpled paper. Maybe the siren wailed for someone for whom all was not lost. The evening darkened. The street lights sprang to life outside the window. Marek resumed his pacing. The music faded away.

It was at this point that I became aware of something that often bothered me about the apartment. The smell. On certain days, it was okay. I didn't notice it at all. But the sudden silence and the darkness awakened me to the smell. I now believe that it was the smell of death. Matthew has convinced me it's all around us, and that there's no escape. My only strength lies in the knowledge that Matthew and I walk hand in hand.

"I was so much in love with her," said Marek, leading me to believe that I must have been speaking to myself, blurting out my innermost thoughts. I watched him stop in front of me. He wiped the tears from his face and lowered himself into the sofa next to me. "What are you going to do now?" he asked.

I could think of nothing to say. A terrible sense of shame swept through my mind as the other face settled before my eyes. It was a shattered, bleeding face, the face of the dying woman. Which was her real face, I wondered. Which was the face I had grown to love? Were they both equally real? The clock ticked away. I was surprised how loud its sound had grown since I last noticed.

I must've been speaking aloud my thoughts again. "It's sometimes impossible to tell which is the more real," said Marek, breaking the silence, "the light or the shadow." We sat for a long time, the old man wrapped in his thoughts, I wondering what his thoughts might be. We heard voices rising from the sidewalk, children's voices and the sound of laughter.

"We were so much younger then," he said, "so full of hope and yet so terrified of life." Marek said his memories were of the time he held Olga's hand and watched a play called *The Post Office*. He lifted a tiny corner of his memory's heavy curtain so I could take a peek.

"I had a reputation in the city, a bad reputation, he said. "So I had to sneak in for the show after the lights went out. Olga was saving a space for me and I knew exactly where to go in the dark. If the city outside was filled with the faint odour of death and disease, the hall inside the orphanage reeked with the stench of urine. The old doctor, Korczak, who ran the orphanage nursed a deep dislike of me. I suspect it was because I often made fun of him in public, muttering stupid rhymes in his face, always trying to pry a few coins off of him. I could make out where he was sitting in front of the audience, his bald head shining in the pale stage lights."

Marek's voice calmed my troubled thoughts. I wanted him to continue. But I interrupted him to ask about his rhymes. "Please tell me some of them. Please."

"They were the stupidest of verses. And I don't remember them."

"That's impossible," I persisted."You never forget anything."

Marek took no notice of my urging. He continued with the memory of Olga and the story. "The room was full of shadows. The shadows moved. It felt as if all the recent ghosts of people murdered in the city had come to watch the play. The shadows deepened as more and more of them seemed to gather by the minute. The shadows were strangely alive. The stage remained empty, but for a young boy from the orphanage who was playing the role of a dying child. Funny how I still remember his name, Abrasha. What looked like shadows only moments ago suddenly sprang to life. Yet, if one thought about it, nothing had changed. Not a single new shaft of light had fallen on the stage, not a single new character had appeared, not a single actor had moved. I can't explain what happened. To this day, I believe shadows are as real as the objects they are shadows of. Now that she is gone, where will I find Olga's shadow? It breaks my heart to think of it. That distant night, the night of the play, even though I held her hand in mine, I felt terribly alone, just as I do now when I know I'll never be able to hold her slender fingers again. They were so soft even fifty years later that one would imagine she grew up a princess. She never grew old in my eyes."

Marek was crying again. For the first time that evening, tears flooded my eyes too. It felt good. But in the back of my mind there sprang the question: which city? whose murders? I had a vague idea it was Warsaw, but I also had a sense - thanks largely to Tom Kerrigan - that the Warsaw Jews got what they deserved. So, later, when we spent our afternoons loitering around the Martyr's Memorial the martyrs didn't interest us half as much as the tourists visiting the memorial.

Marek wiped his cheeks with the back of his hand and continued. "Loneliness must be the fear of not being recognized for who I am. The most terrible loneliness is the fear of not being recognized for a human being. Those of us who lived in this city fifty years ago know that feeling all too well. I suppose I felt lonely watching *The Post Office* because no one, not even Olga who sat next to me, was looking at me. When all eyes are on the stage, for a brief spell the reality of the self is drowned by what happens there. The audience exists in the shadow of the play, the audience becomes the shadow of the play."

"Olga was bringing you some flowers to celebrate," I said. "She was so excited that you had finished your translation."

Marek's head dropped suddenly on his chest. He sighed long and loud, and his whole body seemed to shake.

"We were hoping to hear the play. She even said you had a part for her."

"A flower girl's. But now it's too late."

"I'd still like to hear it," I said. "I know Tetsuo and Connie would like to as well. Perhaps Lydia too." I had no intentions of asking my Martin Fisher whom Marek did not know at this time.

"I suppose so." We remained silent until suddenly he asked me, "Will you help me set up a stage?"

"Of course. But where?"

"Here, right here in this apartment. Simply a place where we can read some parts."

I had no idea why we couldn't just sit around and read. So I simply asked, "When?".

"Tomorrow, perhaps."

But it didn't happen tomorrow. I had many other questions in my mind, but most of all I wanted to ask him more about the play. Somehow I thought it best to wait for tomorrow. I remember every word he said because, on that evening, Marek was already the play and I the audience. It was only later, several months later, that I felt I had the time to understand what Marek was trying to tell me that fateful day in his apartment. I have come to realize that we are all actors and audiences at the same time. I act; you watch, applaud, or turn away. You act, and I do the same.

Marek stopped his monologue just as abruptly as he had started. He had put his arm on my shoulder and somehow touched a spot on my shirt which was wet. I hadn't noticed the spot on the back of my shirt sleeve. Marek didn't need eyes to know it was blood. He asked me to go and change. It didn't matter that he gave me one of his own shirts a few sizes too large for me. All the fear and the shame that had started to drift away suddenly came rushing back at me as I stripped in the bathroom and faced myself in the mirror. It was bad enough Olga was dead, to have her blood on my clothes seemed to brand me as a vicious criminal, however unwitting, in my own eyes if not the eyes of the law. As I washed my arm where the shirt was stained, I realized there was a small gash in my skin as well. Maybe it wasn't Olga's blood after all. Maybe it was mine.

I came out of the bathroom just in time to hear a loud knocking on the door. I opened the door. The police were waiting for me. My first reaction was one of anger rather than fear. I was not their man. At that moment I forgot about friendship, and would have been more than happy to lead them to the real murderer. But I didn't.

Two-Six

Now I was well and truly terrified. Stan and the other kids I would hang out with scoffed at the idea of prison. There was nothing to it, they said. Often, conditions were much worse in their own homes. I realized how wrong they were my very first night in the lock-up. I was holed up in a cell with another inmate, a clean dressed man of about thirty who insisted on laughing in a thin reedy voice every time one of the guards walked past. When the guards weren't around, he would unzip himself and snicker at me while his penis dangled out of his pants like a wilted carrot. In the world outside, we inflict pain and hurt on each other, but there are always plenty of others who are there to heal and comfort, certainly not to hurt. A prison is no sanctuary for the damned, as lawmakers would have us believe. Its very essence is hurtfulness, extreme hurtfulness. It merely perpetuates the pain the inmates inflicted upon others to be thrown into prison in the first place. This was my most terrifying sense of discovery, not the squalor or the soulless physical ugliness of the place. There is no one to turn to, unless it is for a fresh share of pain. I decided that my friends were all washed up. I could see no grounds for their romantic view of prisons.

During the first night in the lock-up, the gash on my left arm bled a little and stained my shirt again. The stain didn't seem to arouse any curiosity in the minds of the officials. Instead, they summoned someone, possibly a doctor, although he looked more like the janitor, to clean up and dress the wound. Olga's face had haunted me all night. What if it was her blood that had first stained my shirt, I wondered. What if our blood had touched and mingled at the gash that Stan had probably

94

inflicted on me during my feeble, half-hearted attempts to save her. It was an exhilarating thought, and I couldn't get any sleep the rest of the night. I kept staring at my arm in the dim light, and the tiny, parted lips of the wound smiled back at me as if charged somehow by a fleeting, ghostly kiss from the dying woman. I almost felt it would sadden me to have the wound heal and the gash disappear.

One of the first things the lawyer warned me against was never to name any names. I took him so literally that, for a while, it seems I simply excised that part of my brain which may be the repository of the names we know. To this day, I often find it very difficult to address people by their names. When I travel, I think what I'll do for place names is write them down on a piece of paper. Of late, I haven't been travelling much, but that's how I think I'll buy rail tickets in the future.

My father's help in getting me out of the clutches of the police was as welcome as it was unexpected. I had not seen him for months, and our last encounter had been anything but pleasant and filial for me. There really isn't too much for which I can feel grateful towards him. For this lawyer I was truly grateful. He was good looking, self-assured, almost cocky. He was wonderful. He must have been expensive too, a rich man accustomed to patronizing others, for his very presence reduced the police and the prison officials to a level of cordiality that I never imagined them to be capable of. "He's only a boy," said the lawyer, pointing towards me, and they nodded in agreement. "He couldn't hurt a fly even if he wanted to," he said again, resting a protective hand on my shoulder. "Give him a break," he added. And they did. For my part, I gave the police no names, just told them how it was my buddy who had bludgeoned the old woman to death with a hammer. I had nothing to do with it, and couldn't even have helped if I wanted to. He was too big, too strong. Yes, they smiled knowingly, for they already had the poor bastard behind bars. This I didn't know at the time. They believed my story. I wanted so much to see Stan, to ask him the same question that had been pounding in Marek's head. Why? But my lawyer quietly brushed aside my request.

One part of me hated Stan for what he had done to Olga, to Marek, and to me. Another part kept remembering the fun times we had had, how he had tried to help out with some of my problems. For, in nineteen ninety four I was only fifteen years old and couldn't imagine I was living through a troubled existence which wasn't common to everyone my age. I kept my problems to myself. In every respect I suppose I was like any other boy growing up in a large city. I played a lot of soccer, I liked my friends, and my friends liked me because I seemed to have more spending money than most of the others. In the evenings, we would often wander up and down Marszalkowska looking into store windows flaunting things we desperately wished for, and ended up buying ice-cream, at my expense of course. Occasionally, I would treat my friends to hamburgers at Burger King. But I always did the hamburgers with my mother's knowledge, and her money. My friends and I loved my mother - whom we'd call the flower lady - very much.

I was glad to have finally found a mother like everyone else. This led me to hope that I could sometimes claim to be like everyone else. What set me apart from the others, though not everyone surely, was a painful inability to understand why some people were less than other people, why they deserved to be excluded from normal society, normal society being of course that to which I and my friends belonged. I have since spent hours trying to analyze this problem in terms of genetics, only to discover, in sheer frustration, that this was a point where the great thinkers departed from genetics and turned to the environment for answers. This wasn't going to be much help to me in prison.

Thanks to my father's and his lawyer's help, I stayed home most of the following week, lapping up Lydia's attention and concern for my well-being. I felt a strong urge to go visit Marek since he didn't have a telephone. Then something new began to happen. From time to time, a piece of music that the two of us had unexpectedly heard in Tetsuo's office began to interrupt my thoughts. Every time the music turned on in my mind, my heart ached for Marek and I wanted to rush out of the apartment. But Lydia wouldn't hear of it. The refrain would come and go as it wished. I seemed to have no power to make it go away.

During my stay at home, the wound healed nicely. But it left behind something, something I would like to call memory. When I showed it to Lydia, at first she tried to scrub it away. She put out a large bowl of warm water in the bathroom, made me strip and had me wash myself from head to foot. It didn't seem to make the slightest difference. Then, armed with a fresh, rougher kitchen towel, she decided to tackle the problem herself. All she succeeded in doing was scraping off the scab and opening the way for fresh drops of blood to ooze out of the skin. The strange emblem that had appeared on my arm, brushed with a lighter pigmentation on my somewhat darker skin, seemed to mesmerize Lydia. When she showed it to my father in the evening, he went into a state that I can only describe as extreme shock. This I found quite unusual, for Martin Fisher was a real tough guy.

Always a man of action, as soon as he had recovered somewhat he promptly decided to send me back home. Addressing me by my usual name, he said, "I'm worried about you here, Matt. You must go back."

I looked at his face, wondering what he was talking about, who he was talking to. He must have noticed the blank expression on my face for he raised his voice somewhat and said, "I'm talking to you."

It took me a moment to wake up and get back on track, I had become so used to the name Misha that Lydia and others used to call me by. "Oh!" I said, adding softly with undisguised contempt, "whatever you say, Dad." Later, I kept wishing I had begged for some time to say my farewells, but the last thing he wanted me to do was go visit Marek.

I think my father felt good about the trouble and expense he had gone to for the sake of his son. But the shock was too much for him. Ultimately, he ended up extracting a price for his benevolence. He sent me back home half way around the world.

You may wonder if this was to be my prison for the next four years, until news of Marek's death brought me back to his apartment. If you do, you'd be wrong.

Two-Seven

Martin was the most rational of human beings, and I was beginning to hate him. Marek never embarrassed me. He was just slightly crazy, but I loved him for it. Through him, I began to meet other old people, not half as crazy, like Olga who - I could tell from our very first meeting - was more the old man's age than my father's. It bothered me to think that someday my father might, just might, become like Marek who had lost the power of sight and didn't walk very well either. Would my heart then reach out to him too? Just for reassurance, I checked this out with Tom Kerrigan, the science teacher from my old school, when I met up with him after my father shipped me home. Mr. Kerrigan was quite confident that such a transformation might not necessarily take place.

"So, Matthew, how did you like your trip abroad?" he asked.

"Warsaw is a big city, as you had told us in class," I replied.

"Now the Communists are gone, we should make a final push to get rid of all Jews."

I was on the verge of telling Mr. Kerrigan that I thought the job was nearly done. According to Marek's count, there were only two hundred and seventy Jews left in the city. I had thought of sending Tom Kerrigan the news, but never got round to it. I had once written out a few lines on a picture postcard showing the old city, but there was too long a line at the post office and eventually I lost the card. As I was preparing to give him the information at the super-market checkout a strange, haunting music suddenly started to play in my mind. So I couldn't tell him what I wanted to. We parted at the check-out and I left him none the wiser. But I'm glad I didn't give him the figure of two hundred and seventy Jews.

That wouldn't have been accurate. To be precise, it should be two hundred sixty nine, but that might be wrong too. Meanwhile, the music had stopped.

Truly, I remember thinking, this man, our junior high science teacher, is an astonishing person who had an explanation for everything. Life, to him, was simply a battle of the genes. Genes determined who won and who lost. Sounded pretty brilliant to me, really amazing stuff. Thanks to him, I was well and truly hooked on genes. Except that the doctor's diagnosis had raised some puzzling questions in my mind, and I was afraid to go back to Mr. Kerrigan. I had really no one to talk to about my condition, and I had not yet started my own extensive study of genes.

My real mother lived, in a manner of speaking, about seventy or eighty miles away. But she was inaccessible. She was crazy too, really crazy. That's why I hardly ever saw her. Sometimes, I wondered whether my father might become like my mother. Worse still, whether I might become like my mother. Many months ago, well before we moved to Europe, the science teacher thought both these possibilities somewhat unlikely. Still, there were moments in my life in Warsaw when I was in such a bad state that I thought quite seriously that Tom Kerrigan must be wrong.

It was particularly bad after Olga's death when nothing seemed to make any sense any more. There were moments when Olga's death filled me with little more than fear. I kept hearing things, seeing faces. They were objects I often failed to recognize, faces to which I couldn't assign names. For instance, if there's one person whose presence I could breathe every time I passed a florist's or walked through a garden, it is the flower lady's. I kept calling her the flower lady out of a force of habit, for in the wake of Olga's death, obviously at a rather delicate point in my life, I felt forbidden to use names. I realize it was for my own good, but the good has probably come and gone, and such is the power of suggestion I still haven't completely shaken off the habit. But I'll try.

I had no reason to remember her back home since I was neither in a garden nor in a flower shop. There are no flower shops in Field, and no one worries about gardens since you'll rarely notice if it's spring or summer it's so brief. In fact, I was sitting in a doctor's office - a pleasant enough waiting room where I kept catching the eyes of the blonde receptionist who could well be the doctor's wife or his mistress. The reason I was reminded of Lydia was because I had just picked up a magazine and turned the pages to a Calvin Klein ad for a men's fragrance which was actually reeking of the smell of lavender. The smell was so strong that I had to put the magazine down. A few more seconds of the fragrance and my sinuses would've choked up for sure. I'm certain they didn't call it lavender, for that would hardly be uncommon. Lydia's fragrance - or fragrances, I should say - were far more subtle. I had no problems with her.

The Calgary dermatologist had been highly recommended not only by our family physician but other satisfied clients as well, so I was told. He turned my arm around, made me lift it above my head, and began to ask me about my sexual habits. I thought he was looking at the wrong place but decided to be patient and answer him. Nothing during the last month or so, I told him. Before that, just about every night, with occasional breaks. Generally with the same person, but sometimes I needed a change just like everyone else. No, the change wasn't indiscriminate; the same person. Just two partners over a period of twelve months.

"And you're only sixteen?" he asked, squinting at the personal details I had jotted down under the receptionist's flirtatious eyes.

"Yes, almost," I nodded somewhat sheepishly.

I didn't like the way his lip seemed to curl up just a little at one end. In fact, I thought I detected a slight hint of contempt in his voice as he finally pronounced his verdict. "Young man, you have a rare case of *Pigmentosa Judaica*," he said. "When did you first notice it?" he asked, taking down quick notes in his file.

It was almost the day after the murder that I noticed this curious thing happening to my right arm. For lack of any other explanation, I thought of it at the time as some kind of skin infection. I kept hoping it would go away. It was not a growth or anything of that sort. Just a patch of whiteness on the skin that started off as a thin but definite circle. Actually, it looked quite cool in the beginning. I felt bothered and self-conscious only when it started to widen and the added blue pigmentation came along. But since I didn't feel compelled to scratch or rub this patch on my skin, I was quite content to keep the condition to myself, until I found the design looking more and more ominous. This was another reason I didn't resist more strongly my father's insistence that I return home. "A couple of months ago," I replied. But I was more interested in cures than in names. "Will it go away?" I asked.

"No," he answered, without looking up from his notes.

"Are you not going to prescribe anything for it?" I asked. "Some cream maybe."

"No," he smiled, "you'll just have to live with it. It's not fatal and I doubt if it's infectious. You're the very first case I've seen. It's rare, very rare." He shut his file with an air of finality.

"I suppose it just looks odd, I said, trying to play down my concern and discomfort. "There's no pain or scratching," I added.

"Oh, it'll come, it'll come," he replied, nodding wisely, smiling superciliously.

I hid my irritation with great difficulty. "Will it spread?" I asked.

"That's hard to tell," he answered, leading me out through the door.

"How does one get it, doctor?" This at least I needed to know.

"There's very little research on the subject, but I suspect it's genetic. I believe you are suffering from a kind of genetic mutation that we call mimicry. For instance, some butterflies mimic the bright external coloration of certain inedible butterflies because that way they might avoid being eaten up by birds. So mimicry is a protective, defensive mode of genetic selection. But I honestly can't see how this is going to help you. Quite ironic, heh! heh!"

I hated his laughter. "Do you sleep with the woman out there, your receptionist?" I suddenly asked, glancing in the direction of the blonde as I stepped out of the examination room. I've had such luck with older women that I wanted to be sure, just in case.

The doctor reddened. I couldn't tell if it was a flush of anger or a blush of embarrassment. He looked thoughtful for a moment, and then started speaking slowly. "You cheeky bastard," he said, "I have a wife and kids."

In retrospect, I think he could have been more forthcoming. But it doesn't matter, I thought, as I smiled goodbye to the woman. I never went back to the office. On my way home in the Greyhound bus, I tried to comprehend what the diagnosis meant for me. I suppose I'd have to cover myself, at least the arms, assuming the condition didn't spread to my face or hands. Thank God it wasn't leprosy, my fingers weren't likely to rot away. Perhaps I should stay away from beaches. No communal bathing in the hot springs. Well, I consoled myself that it was not a death sentence. But why me?

My thoughts became more and more mired in the question as the Calgary-Vancouver bus rolled along. I looked at the inscrutable faces of my fellow travellers and wondered how many of them were probing the same question, why? Why is the other guy blessed with a Mercedes? Why is my boss such a shithead? Why isn't my woman any sexier? Of course, I couldn't tell which of these questions went slithering through whose mind. But it did occur to me that there might be a genetic predisposition to the question why.

And yet, this certainly wasn't a gene I had inherited from my father. Maybe my mother, but I guess I'll never know. And I certainly couldn't have inherited it from Marek Rubenstein unless he had somehow, miraculously, slept with my mother. Marek did raise the question of my mother's culpability on an earlier occasion.

Two-Eight

Martin Fisher promised to join me in ten days time, but the promise meant little to me. Almost from the day I landed at my destination and took a taxi home, it no longer seemed like home to me. Then I began to miss my mother. Most of all, I missed Matthew who seemed to have grown very distant. I missed his friends. I missed Matthew's intellectual toughness, sometimes - though not always - a match for Stan. And I missed Matthew's endless curiosity, so that my own days began to seem dull and boring. When I entered our empty home nestled in a green valley in the shadow of tall snow-covered mountains it seemed I had seen it all, experienced it all. That was not a nice feeling. I felt that I didn't belong to the place any more.

I bought some groceries, vacuumed the house, opened all the windows to drive out the stale smell inside. Much like the smell of old age, though the house had been built long after I was born. Mr. Jensen the grocer was surprised to see me, but asked nothing more than whether my dad too was back, not asking anything else when I said no. People were friendly enough in our little alpine village. They didn't ask too many questions and kept mostly to themselves. In the three years that we had moved away, all my old friends seemed to have moved too. It being the time for school holidays when I came home that summer, some of my old friends might be expected to be away visiting family elsewhere. I could have found out for sure if I needed to, but I didn't feel like it. My mind was somewhere else. I doubt that the murder was beginning to bother me in any way. I thought I had put it out of my mind for good. What did bother me was this music I had first heard with Marek, and often without him since that first time. Now the music followed me everywhere. I couldn't stand on our front yard and look at the mountains without hearing the music. It was in the air. True, the music was kind of beautiful, but why did it play in my ears? It would start off quite unpredictably, like the other day when I ran into Mr. Kerrigan in the village super-market.

One morning I headed out for Burgess Ridge and got there just as a bunch of paleontologists were winding up their day's work. The sunshine on the surrounding peaks was just as splendid as ever. Emerald Lake as inscrutable as before. If there was a faint melody tripping lightly through my mind, by the time I got to Burgess Shale it had hit a crescendo, a roar. It was utterly maddening.

It seemed terrible to be thousands of miles away from everyone who mattered to me. I had to go back and watch Marek's play unfold. I couldn't stay where I was much longer. It was a worse place than any jailhouse I had known. Strange how one can dither for an age and suddenly make up one's mind in a flash. It happened to me when I went looking for the post office to send a letter to Lydia. In the three years that we had been away, it was gone. Now it's in Morgan's Drugstore. How idiotic! That's when I told myself Marek was waiting for me, and Lydia, and Connie and Tetsuo. I had to go.

With his customary foresight and keen sense of economy, my father had bought me, not a one-way ticket home, but a round-trip which helped him save money for some unaccountable reason. I would take out the ticket from time to time and find the return date calling out to me like Eve's irresistible apple in the Garden of Eden. I began to look at the ticket every morning before breakfast only to discover that I was another day closer to succumbing.

In his absence, Martin's letters had kept piling up behind the front entrance. I picked up the mail from the floor dutifully each afternoon and arranged it in neat piles on one side of the kitchen table. Once in a while I would idly examine a letter to see where it had come from. It was such a curiosity that led me to an official looking letter from Bonn which, on closer examination, turned out to be a pension cheque from the German Veterans of War Department. It suddenly dawned on me why, towards the end of every month, Martin would grow more restless than usual as he waited for Jeff the mailman to bring him his letters. Most of the time there was a lot of junk. But at month's end, and sometimes on the first days of the new month, there would be one letter he seemed particularly anxious about. His anxiety would be most pronounced during the winter months when heavy snowfall kept Jeff confined to the post office. Martin would grow more and more stressed as the snow piled up, and I couldn't help thinking how it seemed oddly out of character for him. Curiously enough, his name 'Fisher' was spelt 'Fischer.' In spite of this discrepancy, I was certain the pension cheque was for him and him alone.

But what did Martin do in the war? It was a question that I was never able to ask. Once, during a conversation between him and Marek at their first meeting, the question was at the tip of my tongue. Again, I was cut short as a strong shiver passed through me as Marek said of my father, "He's a wonderful person. We should get to know each other better. We have such a wonderful basis for a friendship. He has fought fires most of his life. And I, during the best years of my life, fed fires."

October 12, 1998

So, I was back in Warsaw, on my own. And they sent me back to prison.

Now it was evening and we were gathered in Marek's place once more. It started on a faint note of disappointment since Tetsuo had forgotten to bring his music. But his enthusiasm for Marek's writing more than made up for this lapse. Since Martin was also in town, it had crossed my mind once to suggest to the others that we invite him too. In the end, my deepest instincts told me he would be out of place in our midst.

We began where we had left off, with the young boy, Amal, reaching out to people outside through the window of his room where he's confined due to illness. I half hoped that we would get closer this night to discovering why Tagore's play meant so much to Marek Rubenstein.

At the customary moment, the wind started to blow and the spirits moved in on us. In the absence of Tetsuo's music, it was the wind that wailed in the background.

[Enter Milkman]

Milkman: *I got some sweet curd. Great stuff! Melts in your mouth.*

Amal: *Hello! Who's there?*

Milkman: *Hello! Would you care for some curd?*

Amal: *How can I? I can't buy any.*

Milkman: *What a drag! I'm just wasting my time then, chatting with you.*

Amal: *Why don't you take me with you?*

Milkman: *You're a strange lad. What're you doing here anyway?*

Amal: *Doctor's orders. I'm supposed to be sick.*

Milkman: *What's the matter with you?*

Amal: *I don't know. I must be stupid. You see, I don't read any books. Where do you live?*

Milkman: *I come from our village on the river Shamli at the foot of the Panchmura hills.*

Amal: *Your village is under some big trees, by the side of the red road, isn't it? Cattle graze*

            on the hillside, and young women draped in red fill their pitchers from the river and

            carry them on their heads.

Milkman: *You've been there, have you?*

Amal: *Only in my dreams. But will you take me there, when I'm better?*

Milkman: *Of course, I will.*

Amal: *And you'll teach me to cry 'curds' and carry the pots on my shoulder like you?*

Milkman: *But why in heaven's name will you sell curds? Surely, you'll read books and grow up to be wise.*

Amal: *No, I'll never be wise. Never. Sorry, I'm keeping you too long.*

Milkman: *Not a bit. You've taught me to be happy selling curds.*

[Exit Milkman]

[Enter Watchman]

Amal: *Ah! Here comes the watchman. Hello Watchman.*

Watchman: *How now? Who dares call out to me?*

Amal: *I do.*

Watchman: *And suppose I march you straight to the King?*

Amal: *Oh! do that, please. Will you? But why don't you sound your gong instead?*

Watchman: *Because my time has not yet come.*

Amal: *How strange. Some say time has not yet come, and others say time has gone by.*

Watchman: *The sound of my gong tells the people: Time waits for none, but goes on forever.*

Amal: *Goes where? To which land?*

Watchman: *That no one knows.*

Amal: *How I wish I could fly with Time to that land which no one knows of.*

Watchman: *All of us must get there someday, my child. You too.*

Amal: *But my doctor won't let me out.*

Watchman: *Maybe the doctor himself will take you there by the hand.*

Amal: *He won't. You don't know him. He only wants to shut me in.*

Watchman: *One greater than he will come and set you free.*

Amal: *When will this great doctor come for me? I can't stand it in here any more . . . . . . Say, what's going on there in that big new house on the other side? There's a flag flying high up and people are always going in and out.*

Watchman: *Oh! there? That's our new post-office,* **dakghar.**

Amal: *Post-office? Whose?*

Watchman: *Whose? Why, the King's, surely!*

Amal: *But who will fetch me my King's letter when it comes?*

Watchman: *The King has many postmen. Haven't you seen them running around with round badges on their chest?*

Amal: *Ah! How I want to be the King's postman when I grow up. Of course, you do a fine job too. When it's silent everywhere in the noon-day heat, you sound your gong. And some-times, when I suddenly wake up at night and find the lamp blown out, it's good to hear you sounding your gong through the darkness.*

Watchman: *Thanks. But here comes the Headman. I must be going. He mustn't find me chatting when I'm supposed to be working.*

[Exit Watchman]

Amal: *Won't it be great to have a letter from the King every day? I'll read the letters at this window. Oh dear! I can't read. But Auntie reads her "Ramayana." Maybe she can help me read the King's writing. If not, I'll read them when I grow up. But what if the postman can't find me ..... Mr. Headman! May I have a word with you?*

[Enter Headman]

Headman: *"Who's yelling after me in the street? You, you little brat?*

Amal: *Sir, will you please tell the postman it's Amal who sits by the window.*

Watchman: *What's the good of that?*

Amal: *Just in case there's a letter for me from the King.*

Watchman: *What a presumptuous little fellow you are! A letter from the King?*

Amal: *You sound annoyed. Are you cross with me?*

Watchman: *Cross indeed. Madhav has grown too big for his boots. He's made a little pile for himself and now kings and lords are common folk to him. I'll make sure the King's letter gets to your house. Indeed, I will. I'll tell the King about you, and he won't be long. One of his postmen will come presently with news for you.*

[Exit Watchman]

Amal: *Who are you walking by? The bells on your feet ring so sweetly.*

[Enter Sudha]

Sudha: *I'm Sudha, daughter of the flower-seller. I gather flowers in my basket.*

Amal: *Oh! gathering flowers. That's why your feet seem so glad and the bells jingle so happily as you walk. Wish I could be out too. Then I'd pick you some flowers, the ones which hide behind the topmost branches, the ones beyond your reach. I know the fable of Champa and her seven brothers. So, if only they'd let me, I'd go right into the deep forest where you could easily lose your way. There, where the honey-sipping humming-bird rocks himself on the end of the slenderest branch, I'd blossom into a 'champa'. Will you be my sister, Parul?*

| Sudha: | *You're silly. How can I be your sister Parul when I'm Sudha? I must go, for I have many garlands to weave today. Be good, and on my way back home with the flowers, I'll stop by and chat with you.* |

[Exit Sudha]

[Enter Boys]

Amal:	*Say, where are you guys off to?*
A Boy:	*We're going to play at being ploughmen.*
Amal:	*Please don't go. Why don't you play on the street near this window? I could watch you then. Here are my toys, Take them. They are getting dirty and are of no use to me. I can't play alone.*
A Boy:	*Thanks. We'll stay. Let's stand these soldiers in a line. We'll play war games instead. But where can we get a gun? Ah, here! this reed will do nicely. But you seem half asleep already.*
Amal:	*I'm afraid I'm very sleepy all of a sudden.*
A Boy:	*Listen. The gong's sounding the first watch. Time we were off.*
Amal:	*Before you go, tell me something. Do you know of the King's postmen? I'm waiting for a letter.*

A Boy:	*We know them for sure. One's Badal, the other's Sarat. If your name's on the letter one of them will surely find you.*
Amal:	*Please come back tomorrow and point them out to me.*
Boys:	*We will. Good-bye now.*

[Exit Boys]

* * * * *

"Let's stop here for the night, please," said Connie.

"I'm grateful to you for doing this for me," said Tetsuo, turning to look at me and then at Connie. "You don't know how much it means to me."

"Perhaps it'll help me too," I murmured, "help me break away from Marek's spell. Finally, we seem to have found the post-office. What happens next?"

Connie stretched herself and threw an arm over Tetsuo's shoulder. "Are you prepared to pay the price of another dinner for tonight's reading?" she asked him.

"She's not from L.A.," laughed Tetsuo, pointing towards Connie. "She must be from Transylvania. These expensive dinners will get me fired from my job. I'll be dead."

"Undead," corrected Connie.

The wind became silent and the moonlight spilled onto the empty floor.

October 13, 1998

I had no idea that the third day of my freedom would turn out to be one of the most intense in my entire life. The enigmas of the previous evening's reading of the play still fresh in my mind, I was trying to focus on the day that lay ahead when the doorbell rang. Somewhat unhappy over being dragged out of bed, it didn't take long for Tetsuo's voice on the intercom to drive away my irritation.

Tetsuo handed me a packet. "It came to me from your father," he said. He looked oddly agitated as he added, "It came with a brief note addressed to no one in particular." He handed me an open envelope with the note.

I unfolded the message and read: "Consider me a victim of the millennium bug. I'm tired of hiding in my safe haven in the mountains. I have decided I don't deserve to walk into the twenty-first century. I belong so much to this century of hate and deception, of murder and lies, that I have nowhere else to go."

"That's it?" I asked, looking up at Tetsuo.

"Yes," he nodded.

"Where has he gone?"

"Can't say yet."

The message was worrisome, but there was little to do but wait. Neither Tetsuo nor I dared ask the other what it is that my father meant. I once considered summoning supernatural aid by mumbling the words *Adair, Adair*. But the thought appeared foolish on this day, and so I set it aside.

I felt distracted. I remembered that during the night I had dreamt of Stan. Now, it seemed I had already made up my mind in my half sleep to go looking for him. Tetsuo shook me back to reality. "Aren't you going to open the packet?" he asked.

"No," I replied firmly, "not just yet." Then, trying to sound a little more caring, I asked, "Do you know what it is?"

"Yes, it's a manuscript."

I couldn't help smiling as I remembered something. "You know what he thought of you?" I asked.

"Yes," Tetsuo smiled back. looking embarrassed. "We'll talk about that later." With that he took his leave.

"We'll see you this evening, won't we?" I remembered to call out to him from the stairwell. "Don't forget the music."

"I won't," he shouted back.

Once inside, I thought of making myself some breakfast and then decided against it. There was a pot of coffee from the previous night. I poured it into a saucepan, lit a gas fire under it, and let it heat.

While I waited, I felt drawn once more to Marek's papers. It amused me to think that, only after two days, it was becoming something of a ritual for me to start the morning with a look at his diary. It was grey and gloomy outside, and I had to switch on the lights before I could read anything.

But for some boxes piled up on the floor, the place looked not much different from before. I felt a momentary excitement imagining that Marek might suddenly appear from one shadowy corner or the other and it would be the same as before. I still had so much to tell him.

The somewhat stale smell of coffee rose from the stove as I browsed through one of his diaries and stopped at a random page. Yes, it was becoming a habit, like a morning conversation with Marek. And then our readings in the evening!

I couldn't help asking myself if I was becoming prisoner to a system. Marek would surely have chided me for that. But plays, I remembered, do come to an end. And so must our gatherings.

"Tell me about this play of yours," I finally ended up asking him one day. "What's it about, some kind of post-office?"

"No," he replied, "it's about a lie. The post-office is a lie."

"What do you mean?" I persisted.

"You'll find out some day, after I'm done with the translation," he said. "I love Tagore, but I detest the play because it asks you to put your faith in a lie."

THREE

And it struck me one day that the deadliest plagues are those of the mind. There's no vaccine, no antidote that can protect one against them. All one can do is wash one's hands like Pontius Pilate and hope to remain untouched by the canker. But that's an exercise in futility, because it's not the hands that are the first to go, but the mind. No amount of washing and scrubbing can cleanse the mind. So, what can?

Fool that I am, I have spent my life pondering the question. Fools have faith in foolish things, and it may be that some good will come out of my foolishness. I must believe in something. I did believe in something when I was a child. It used to be small parts of something whose wholeness I was too young to understand. Like pillars of marble and malachite which I could touch and feel, but could not see the massive roof it held aloft. It was a world I trusted, a world in which I felt completely safe as I ran around the enormous nave and apse of the main prayer hall. When scolded for my lack of respect and manners, I would wrap my arms around one of the two beautiful dark-veined marble columns at the apse entrance and pretend to look contrite, and my mother would gather me in her arms and the matter would end there. It felt so warm to belong to a throng of a thousand worshippers, staring in wide-eyed wonder at the ark which held the Torah and the rabbi, his tallith on his head, reading at the bimah. And Rabbi Samuel Poznanski who translated the prayer book into Polish, so it could be used by the so-called assimilated gentlemen who wore top hats to religious services. To what end, I ask myself?

Ah! the Synagogue on Tlomackie. We tried so hard to win the love of others. We copied, we borrowed. The majesty of the porticoed central section, the dome, the receding wings, and the buildings projecting from the end - details which went back to the church of St. Charles Borromeo in Vienna and the Palace of Justice in Brussels. To think that we stole ideas from the Oranienburgerstrasse Synagogue in Berlin to win acceptance in the eyes of others, to please others.

Then the plague blew its foul breath and, on Crystal Night in 1938, Berliners who regarded the Jews of Berlin as an inferior Oriental race set fire to the Moorish synagogue.

The true nature of the plague that wiped out almost all of us is the mystery that has consumed my mind these past fifty years or more. The rabbis, the saints, the sages, none of them know the answers. Even the poets have failed me. My friend, Dr. Korczak imagined the poet Tagore had some answers, and so decided to stage his play, "The Post Office", in the final hours of his life. He said he had seen Tagore in a dream. I never saw him, in the flesh or in a dream, but I knew every word he ever wrote. If he was looking for answers in Tagore, I think Korczak was wrong. If he was looking for the path ahead, he was dead right.

> *Christ rose from the dead,*
> *Went straight to heaven.*
> *Six million Jews lost their way,*
> *Wound up in Hitler's oven.*

va-y'chulu ha-shamayim (and the heavens collapsed, and the earth as well).

va-yidom Aharon (and Aaron was silent).

* * *

Voice Three: Martin

Three-One

Thereere was something else here. I don't remember, possibly something unimportant. But there were only four principal voices to sing the glory of the Son of God. There's no room for a fifth. So this will be Martin's. I know it is out of place. I'll let it be, just the same.

I had a chance to look through his manuscript several days later, after I had returned to prison. That's when I made up my mind that this distraction, this voice, must be his. But first, there was the unfinished business of Stan in my dreams the night before. I should let Stan intrude as he did most violently later in the day.

Mr. Nowakowski who, as a lawyer, was supposed to have all the answers, proved somewhat evasive about Stan when I had enquired of him some days ago. I didn't press him any further. On this morning, out of prison, I decided to start with the most logical place. I headed for Stan's mother's apartment.

The memory of my first visit to her place returned to me. Why? I'm not certain. Perhaps it was, as on that occasion, the sense of some mysterious encounter which made my body tremble. I was about to come face to face with a healer, a soothsayer, a witch, a *chovihanis*, whose reputation and fortune in the city of Warsaw rested upon a monument of spells, charms, fortunes told and other feats of magical proportions she had helped unlock for her countless believers.

I was expecting to be blown over by a flood of colours, by the glitter and sparkle of gold jewelry and beads. I held my breath as I heard someone approach the door from inside the apartment. Many coats of green lay plastered over the wooden door, clad on one side with a heavy steel plate pierced with holes for, not one, but three keys as usual. I waited as the footsteps stopped on the other side. No doubt someone was trying to see who I was through the peephole a little above the level of my head. I stepped away from the door, imagining that my height made it difficult for me to be seen through the hole.

Then she made me go through a rather unusual routine. She had me take off all my clothes and stand naked while she walked around me, examining me closely. It never occurred to me that she might want to touch me, and she never did. All the while, I felt sort of detached from my body as my eyes took in specific details of the room. In fact, my eyes went scavenging through the dark room, and I remember pieces of silk waving from the walls, the ceiling, and cushions made of patches of silk strewn all around the room. There was the musty smell of a tomb, and I wondered if Stan's mother was in hiding.

"I was in hiding for a long time," she said, "hiding in the forests like we hid from the Nazi *Einsatzgruppen* hunting expeditions. Now we feel a little more safe, but I've grown used to the darkness and lost all interest in the bright outdoors."

Later, I asked her why she had asked me to strip. She never answered me directly, but told me the strange story of Catherine the Great once observing a tall, dirty, bedraggled and bearded Gypsy walking the street below her window.

She asked Prince Potemkin to summon the Gypsy to her palace. An hour later the Gypsy was brought before the Queen. He was dressed not in rags, but in courtly garments. He was bathed, shaven, and sprinkled with perfume. Catherine was furious. "I wanted him as he was," she cried, "Not as he is now."

The Gypsy looked squarely at Catherine and, recalling to Catherine her humble origin under which he remembered her, said, "I too have wanted you as you were, not as you are." Angered by such impertinence, Catherine ordered that the Gypsy be stripped nude and made to stay outdoors overnight, chained to a warmly dressed soldier. At night, the temperature dropped to forty degrees below zero. In the morning, when Catherine came out to see what had happened, she found the soldier dead while the naked Gypsy was snoring contentedly beside him.

On this day, she readily opened the door for me. I was expecting a warm welcome. Instead, I was surprised by the unmistakable look of terror on her face the moment our eyes met. We tried to make polite conversation. After all, we hadn't seen each other in nearly five years.

"Why did you come back to Warsaw?" she asked. "They did let you get away to Canada, didn't they?"

"Yes," I replied, "but something inexplicable drew me back to this place."

She tried to sound cheerful, enticing a certain brightness to her wrinkled face. "You've grown quite a lot, haven't you?"

I remembered I was considerably smaller in comparison to Stan five years ago. Foolishly, I asked, "Has Stan grown too?"

"No," she said, "he's just the same, wild as ever. Who knows, one day someone might accuse him of roasting alive and eating Polish children."

"When can I see him?" I asked.

"He'll be home for lunch, but not any earlier."

If only I could re-create one more time the carefree afternoons of the past, idling away on park benches, observing passers-by, commenting on the girls. "Maybe he could meet me at our familiar spot off Anielewicza," I suggested. "I'll wait for him there after one,"

"I'm so happy to see you," she said, "but I also wish you hadn't come. The earlier look of fear returned to her face, but I stopped short of asking her why.

"There has been so much unhappiness," she said in farewell. I was starting to walk away from her door when I heard her say that.

"What do you mean?" I asked, turning to face her one more time.

"Look at me," she said. "What do I have except this fatal gift? Nothing. Last night I heard an owl cry and cry over my window. We are doomed. Nobody pities us, nobody mourns us, nobody will remember us. Stan will go the way hundreds of thousands of others have, our own flesh and blood, and nobody will take notice." She moved a step closer to me. "I'll make sure Stan is dressed in his finest clothes." She smiled. "This is my secret," she said, placing her finger on my lips. "It will be yours too."

Three-Two

For a long time I believed that prison is the only place where one can study, and more importantly, one can write. The four walls become increasingly familiar each day. First, I began to see the different shades of white and grey, quite indistinguishable during my first days, on the walls. They changed their colour as the light changed outside, almost every hour, noticeably different in summer than during the winter months. Next, I was able to see spots where the paint had peeled off, only to be covered over with a thick coat of dust which I never disturbed after the first time my finger touched one and it felt like I was disturbing a grave which is something I have not actually done. Finally, I was able to see through the paint and read the outlines of names - perhaps of other prisoners or their loved ones - and also poems, curses and obscenities, faded epitaphs to loneliness. From here, a gradual transition to a constriction of the mind appears inevitable. Like a constriction that forces a vein to pop and burst, memories, people, incidents I had forgotten began unexpectedly to surface in my mind, sometimes in my sleep, often when awake. Thoughts abandoned by the wayside in my youth sprang to life and demanded to be recognized. The fog of mystery lifted from the once inscrutable behaviour of others. Only the music evaded all explanation, the music that came and went like birds in a garden, with a will of its own.

Left to my own devices in the outside world, I would never have thought there were so many words within me. If they hadn't physically locked me up behind bars, I wonder how I could have ever unburdened myself. I suppose one could isolate oneself from the rest of the world, but that is pure hogwash, make-believe. You might as well believe that one can dream oneself into writing. But since there are obviously many writers who never went to prison, I forced myself to think long and hard about how they might have done it.

Marek never held me responsible for Olga's death. He continued to see me. In the beginning, it was Lydia who brought him. Later, it was mostly Connie. The women brought me books, chocolates, and cookies but said very little. Without meaning to, Marek always ended up dominating the conversation. My father would come once in a blue moon, and always complained about the sloppiness of the prison. "These guys have no organizational skills," he lamented. "How can you run a government if you can't run a prison?" I never liked his visits, for he used every opportunity to emphasize how much the visit cost him in time and effort.

Marek was obviously a writer, although what precisely he was writing remained a mystery to me for a long time. A play, yes; but there are plays, and then there are plays. After listening carefully to my thoughts about prison and writing, he finally put my anxieties to rest. He assured me it had nothing to do with being free or being in prison. On the contrary, it had everything to do with the imagination which was, as he put it, like a self-impregnating organism. It was a bit like bees, ants and wasps, he said, adding, "But don't ask me to explain any further."

I didn't think bees, ants, and wasps were a part of Marek's intellectual repertoire. I was told that for a long time he taught an Eastern language at the University of Warsaw, until the German authorities banned all non-Aryan subjects and books. I did notice several books on alien religions on his shelves. But his teaching days were long past by the time I came to know Marek Rubenstein. When I asked him why he didn't resume teaching after the war, he said he was no longer a teacher, only a lucky fool who had survived the war. "People looked strangely at you," said Marek, "as if to ask; what did you do to survive the war. Besides, the wells of my knowledge had been sucked dry."

Marek never wanted to speak about those lost years of his life, as he described the time. But he did volunteer random details occasionally. He had been among a handful of prisoners who escaped when, in a final act of desperation, a band of dying and half-dead Jews set fire to the Treblinka Death Camp. He took days to trudge back to Warsaw, hiding during the day in gutters and the fringes of deserted villages along the way. Then he took up shelter in the Jewish cemetery between Smetna and Okopowa Streets, sometime in the summer of 1943. By then, the Ghetto had been reduced to rubble and the burials were few and far between. There were hardly any Jews left to bury. So the cemetery proved a perfect hiding place for months. The odd benefactor would leave some food in the cemetery even as they came to say their prayers for the dead. The cemetery was known to be hiding some fugitives.

There was a single fugitive whom he met one day, a Jew like himself, with whom he became friends. He asked me, said Marek, what I did before. "I told him," said Marek, "that a long time ago I taught people to read, but that of late I had been thinking of teaching Jewish children to pray. Ah! replied the stranger, then heaven must have sent you to me. Teach me a prayer. Which one? I asked. The Kaddish, he said. For whom? I asked. For my children, he replied; for their mother, for their friends, for all the lies I believed in, for my withered life."

They were still hiding in the cemetery when, in the Spring of 1944, the two had ventured out one evening near Leszno Street. "We weren't prepared for what we saw in the empty ground of the Ghetto. For a moment it looked like heavenly apparitions finally coming down to earth. But no, from their black priests' habits we recognized them to be the Salesian fathers who had often helped to hide Jews. They were six of them hanged from wooden posts. They were still swinging there the next evening when we dared go out for another look.

"My friend said to me that night, 'Let us go away from here.' Where can we go, I asked. 'It hardly matters,' he said, 'as long as we get away from this cemetery.' And he listened while I explained to him what an impossible situation we were in. For in those days, it seemed the whole world had become a cemetery. And I told him how, in Treblinka, I had seen cemeteries in the sky as well, grey cemeteries laden with monuments of ashes, reverberating with the cries of the dying in Treblinka which were like hymns to the dead buried in the sky."

I doubt if Marek would ever have shared these details with me had I not told him about the scepticism of my science teacher. "Tell your teacher that I helped place thousands of Jewish women on iron grates so that billowing flames would melt the last vestige of a smile from their faces. They were beautiful women with glowing bodies and young children who could light up the poorest homes. They were also older men like Janusz Korczak whose bodies were worn and tired. They weren't on the way to the spa. They were dead. Murdered in cold blood. Not in the imagination of this old fool, but in houses that were made to look pretty, with laurelled gates and flower beds and music played in leafy arbours."

Marek's descriptions dealt something of a blow to the methods of scientific enquiry and empirical evidence to which Mr. Kerrigan believed he had inducted his class. Still, his comments about bees and wasps fired my imagination as much as my intellectual curiosity.

At first they would bring me books in alphabetical order. Alexander, Allee, Ardrey, Axelrod, Bastock, Bell, Broadbent, Cairns-Smith, Charnov, Daly, and so on. My excitement over the subject exploded with Darwin. After that, I devoured everything that I could lay my hands on, everything from Dawkins to Maynard-Smith to Zahavi. But here I faced an inner conflict. On the subject of the origin of the species, Marek claimed the credibility of a first-hand witness. I knew he was busy writing something. Could it be that he was about to expound some unique theory of his own? He wouldn't tell me. On the other hand, I believed in Marek implicitly.

On one of those rare occasions when Marek and my father actually met one another while visiting me, my father quite predictably brought up the question of dangerous and dys-functional practices in the Polish prison system. There was filth all around, nobody searches for weapons, no profession-alism. "They ought to search women in particular," he said. "Have you seen the hardware they put inside women's bras these days? Why, you could hide an Uzi in there and smuggle it into the prison and no one would know." Marek agreed with him. He even went so far as to say that no one had shown as much imagination as the Germans in running prison systems. This immediately endeared him to my father whose unshake-able admiration of Germany was closely tied to his equally unshakeable faith in the German mark, the speculative worship of which had helped him become quite a wealthy man. My father felt so expansive about Marek that he expressed his regrets at not having met him sooner, and chided me for not arranging an earlier introduction.

To this day I am not sure whether Marek was having fun at my father's expense or whether he was serious. But there did develop a friendship of sorts between them. In any case, with my new-found love for genetics, I dug deep into the literature and discovered that the nests of bees and wasps have only one mature queen. She mates gloriously but only once when she is young and stores up her sperms for the future. Which means no further sex for the rest of her life which can last as long as ten years. The queen doles out the sperms to her eggs periodically during her long life and some of her eggs get fertilized in the process. But the eggs that don't get fertilized don't wither away. They develop into males. It was at this point that Marek's words began to make sense to me. Male ants, male bees, male wasps don't have any fathers. The cells in their bodies contain only a single set of chromosomes instead of a double set like you and me. [I must confess I'm not totally certain about myself on this point.] It felt good to have worked out this answer, for my words do indeed pour out of me, lost and fatherless like me. The profound realization appeared as beautiful as my memory of the morning's soft autumnal sunshine lighting up the tops of trees outside Lydia's apartment - yellow blossoms and red apples on a green canvas set against a dark sky - the absence of which has been the most excruciating deprivation for me in prison. It feels good to know that, perhaps, I am the real mother.

Marek had been as much a comfort to me in prison as Connie. For a while I think she went back to being Tetsuo's lover, but now she claims she is waiting for me, and only for me. She often travels to Los Angeles on business, but then that's part of her job. When she comes, she simply sits beside me, holds my hand, and says little. Marek tells her that silence is sometimes the highest expression of honesty. Tetsuo comes to visit me too, but he is a quieter man, much more introspective than when I first met him. But it is Lydia that my heart goes out to, my dearest flower lady, whom I miss the most. Lydia looks ill, and her visits are becoming more and more infrequent. About two months ago she brought me a dobosch cake she had baked. This surprised me no end, because I could hardly remember when she last baked for me.

"It's been a long time, hasn't it?" she asked, as I sunk my teeth into a large wedge and drooled over the alternating layers of hard caramel and soft cream.

"Why do you cry?" I asked.

"It's nothing," she said, brushing aside my question with a sad smile.

I suppose they all feel sorry for me. But the judge said he hadn't seen me sorry for my crime. He hadn't seen me cry. There were no grounds for mercy.

"What good is mercy?" I asked him. "It should flow through the gutters for those who need it most, but it doesn't." I did not know what mercy meant aside from what our teacher told us it meant to Shylock in 'The Merchant of Venice'. I could find no regrets in me. The judge looked sternly at me and said, "So be it."

The judge's remarks and my own reaction to them surfaced unexpectedly in my mind a month or so ago after a most unpleasant visit from Mr. Mansell. He seemed to have lost practically all his hair since I knew him last. Still immaculately dressed, there was a sickly yellow pallor on his face. He looked awful. It was obvious all he wanted to do was spite me. He showed up for less than a minute or two, spitting all his venom at me just before he left. "Misha, you little bastard," he said, "go and sleep with Lydia. You'll find the universe gift-wrapped between her thighs. Your Mars, Jupiter, Saturn, the whole fucking works." Then he was gone.

I was astounded. Then a strange thing happened. I began to hear melodies from Holst's *Planets* in my mind. It made me forget everything for the time being. I felt so much at peace.

Lydia didn't visit me in prison after that, so that I had no occasion to ask her what was going on. Marek thought Mansell was but a piece of shit and told me to forget the incident ever happened. I did just that, put it behind me, to my immense regret.

So I have spent a lot of time in prison. What my age is today I have really no idea. Prison has added many more than four years since the day I entered the place. But now I am ready for the world. I have no further reason to hide myself from others. The curious patch of white and blue on my arm, whose discovery by others was my greatest fear before entering prison, still shines defiantly on my skin. It quickly became a joke in prison until one day a maniac sat on me and decided to brand the numbers 007 on my wrist with a red hot needle. While I screamed and before others came to my rescue, he had succeeded in branding the two zeros on my wrist. The other prisoners were more protective of me from then on. As for me, I decided I could live with the two zeros, the sum total of two of life's greatest events, being conceived and lying dead. I have often wondered what life outside holds in store for me, how many more zeros I would earn as feathers to adorn my cap.

I think of retribution too, more so because I continue to believe in my own innocence. And also because I'm convinced Martin Fisher might possibly have committed certain unspeakable crimes during the war for which he decided to drop the "c" from Fischer. An accomplice? An accomplice to what? Am I having to suffer God's punishment? Does God ever dream of retribution before carrying it out? I am convinced there is no joy in the mere dream of retribution - either by God or by man - for one suspects that the hand of God must be somewhat weary. Of course, there could be other reasons for His weariness. Maybe He is still catching His breath after the seventh day, or the sixth depending on which book you read, or maybe He has His hands full simply trying to manage all that He has let loose on the face of the earth. I think Marek must have unconsciously schooled me in these thoughts.

But Marek could also be outrageous and absurd. In a booming voice which the guards and all other visitors could hear, the first thing Marek said on his first visit to the prison was: "Many of them that sleep in the dust of the earth shall awake, some to everlasting life, and some to everlasting shame and contempt. Book of Daniel." Then he burst out laughing and cried, "You are dead, man. You are dead." It was quite unlike Marek to lose control of himself. But he was seeing me after a long time, and perhaps he was trying to overcome some awkwardness. Only once before had I seen him out of control, or so I thought at the time. After a moment of unease and uncertainty the guards supervising the visitors turned their attention to other matters and everyone simply shrugged off the outburst.

On another occasion, Marek reminded me of what he had said on that visit. "Don't believe a word of what I told you," he said. "All is emptiness and hollow. Nothing satisfies, and although the wise excel the foolish, one event happens to them all on this treadmill of time where there is nothing to separate men from beasts in ultimate destiny. Better dead than alive, best of all unborn." He called it the pessimism of Koheleth and, afterwards, asked me to throw that into the garbage as well.

I laughed and assured him our genes would be horrified at the idea of being unborn, for genes are the true immortals, I reminded him. This was something I had learnt in prison. Through trickery or mimicry, if not through natural means, life had to go on. And I gave him the example of birds who are fooled into incubating cuckoo's eggs laid in their nests. They are fooled to the point where the foster-parents continue to feed young cuckoos, almost fledged but considerably larger than the parents, so that the parent sometimes perches on the child's back to feed it. Are the foster-parents stupid? No, what I have understood is that something in the gene of cuckoos has the same effect on the host's nervous system as an addictive drug would have on ours. Genes play all kinds of havoc, all kinds of magic, to see that life goes on. I stopped short of discussing with Marek similar conclusions I had reached in researching my own skin condition. I was increasingly certain I had become host to a parasitic gene which had the same effect on women as the Spanish Fly, a known aphrodisiac. I'm convinced that's the reason women, especially older women, found me so irresistible. My skin condition, which never irritated me, gave them an itch, but had no such effect on men. Which might explain why I avoided getting raped in prison. I befriended no one in prison, no one tried to befriend me.

But Marek caught on to what I was getting at. "You may be right," he said, remembering his experiences in the Warsaw Ghetto. The hooded eyelids covered his blind eyes as he slowly formed his thoughts. "Perhaps Jewishness is an addiction too. Why else would the Germans come down so hard on women caught without the white armbands with the Star of David. They didn't want the flower of German manhood to succumb to the guiles of Jewish women. They were commanded to avoid them like the plague. As if to drive home the point the S.S. asked new recruits if they knew how best to make Jewish women pregnant. The answer: masturbate on a table and let the flies do the rest."

However repulsive the image, I couldn't help marvelling at the brilliance of German geneticists who had so accurately surmised that Jewish women were the greatest barriers to the Final Solution. It was not enough to kill all Jewish males, especially the young robust ones. Of course, what first led me down this trail of wasps, ants, and bees was Marek's observation about the imagination. And this, in turn, led me to ambrosia beetles. I was amazed to discover that Dr. Mengele, a very religious person who had applied genetic theory explaining haplodiploid births to the story of the virginal conception, had also stumbled upon these beetles. That is to say, Dr. Mengele speculated that the precarious survival of the Jewish race, lurching from one catastrophe to the other, depended on something similar to ambrosia beetle eggs that carry a parasitic gene which penetrates unfertilized eggs and helps generate male beetles, fatherless male beetles. Always males. In Auschwitz, Mengele, slowly growing mad with desperation, was ripping up wombs to discover precisely this kind of parasite to stamp out every possibility of the survival of the Jewish gene pool.

My discussions on this subject endeared me to Marek. "I am proud of you," he said. "Prison is good for the soul. I can't wait for you to come out." On that occasion, Martin Fisher happened to be present too. He warmed up to the subject and prefaced his comments with the disclaimer, "I don't want you to think that I am condoning the murder of millions of Jews." Then he went to great lengths to describe how processes and industries evolve, how processes become interlinked, how spin-offs and diversification take place. These were new terms for me and, for the first time, my father amazed me with the clarity of his explanations, until Lydia started to cry and had to go outside.

When she was sufficiently composed to return, Martin told us what he described as a funny story that he had suddenly remembered. It was the tale of Archbishop Hatto of Mainz. There was starvation in the land. The people were bitter and clamouring for food, until Hatto had had enough. He had the beggars rounded up and locked in a barn which he then set on fire. Rid of the peoples' complaints at last, he told the burghers, "Listen to my mice squeaking," as he rubbed his hands in satisfaction. But then a host of mice came streaming out of the barn. They chased Hatto into the tower at Bingen, a lovely village on the Rhine, where they unceremoniously ate him up.

"I can hear the mice, I can hear the mice," murmured Marek as the story ended. Everyone laughed, but I doubt if any one of us truly understood him.

"I think Matthew will understand me," said my father, referring to my scientific interests, "but the German prison system was nothing more than a diversified industry for the protection of good genes and the isolation of the bad, which is exactly the way we see our prison systems today." He pointed out how many of the Nazis were well meaning and only wanted to ease the burdensome existence of those who couldn't fend for themselves. All they wanted to do was save us from lives unworthy of life. "Did you know that well over a quarter million Germans were themselves subjected to compulsory sterilization during the Third Reich - people with mental illnesses, physical disabilities, hereditary problems such as alcoholism and habitual criminality? These were Germans, not Jews or Gypsies."

We sat around in silence. Marek showed no emotion. Lydia had a distant look in her eyes. The guards, who must have picked up some of our conversation, met my gaze with total incomprehension and indifference and kept their eyes away. Finally, Marek cleared his throat and asked, "Would blindness warrant sterilization?"

"Only if it was hereditary," answered my father with an adroitness that probably comes from serious study of the subject, a study which I never had occasion to observe since I saw so little of my father. He continued, "Don't get me wrong. Industries have to evolve, from sterilization you go to euthanasia, from x-ray machines you evolve naturally to the CAT-Scanner and MRI machines. And that's precisely what happened in Germany. I am sorry to say it had to start with children, in hospitals, through forced starvation or fatal medication. Then came a far more extensive programme of adult euthanasia coordinated by a Berlin headquarters known as "T4" and carried out through carbon monoxide gassing. Public reaction forced Hitler to stop this programme in 1941, but he couldn't put the genie back in the bottle. Through a programme known as "Operation 14f13" teams of T4 doctors fanned out to the concentration camps where the volume of prisoners was starting to get out of hand. Sound operations management principles demanded that the system not be allowed to disintegrate. This is how industry keeps pace with change, and the prison industry is no exception. What do you do when you get too many prisoners on Death Row? Do you let them go free? No, you try every way to speed up their execution."

Nobody said anything to continue the discussion. Martin explained how industry leaves no stone unturned in its search for innovation. Why, the Germans even went to private industry to borrow technology, - in fact, to one of the greatest Jewish scientists, the Nobel Laureate Fritz Huber, whose company had perfected the manufacture of Xyklon-B.

"I know," said Marek. "They used Xyklon-B in Auschwitz." It was at this point that Lydia started to cry again, and Martin had to take her out. Marek looked pensive. He spoke softly to me, "I now know Dr. Korczak thought deeply about euthanasia, replete with silent contracts and flowers and pre-selected requiems. He said you wouldn't have to sign any contracts. The contract lies locked in the eyes. Adina was the clever one. Her name was Adina Blady-Szwajger. She fulfilled her contracts at the hospital with morphine. Her patients died with their eyes closed. I wonder if Korczak had given any thought to technology."

"And what did prison do for you?" I asked, somewhat stupidly because I knew many of the details already, including Marek's deep admiration of Dr. Janus Korczak, whom he sometimes described as a martyr-witness in the tradition of

Job and sometimes as a fool. I was merely trying to steer the conversation away from a depressing topic, for I knew why Lydia was crying. I was hoping Marek would respond with something frivolous.

"For one," he said, "my prison taught me that you must be absolutely wrong about Adam and Eve." Marek was commenting on my suggestion, in the course of our discussions, that Eve was formed asexually from Adam's body, so that Eve's body would possess precisely the same characteristics as that of Adam, with some fortunate mutations. "They rose from the swamp," he said, "and I know where it is."

However much I wanted to accept the truth or probability of what Marek said, there was a part of me that remained skeptical. For a long time I believed I had inherited some of my mother's madness and some of my father's fierce independence. With my meagre knowledge of genes I supposed I was half crazy from my mother's side and half the confident, physically powerful man that my father was. My subsequent studies in prison told me I was all wrong. There was no way parents could give us anything but their chromosomes. No wisdom, no knowledge, no faith, no love, no God. We have got to start from scratch and it's always an unequal race.

Do I create Frankenstein in my own image? We can add lightning from the sky to cadavers drawn from earth and create wonders or disasters. But it seems to me those wonders or disasters can be no different from the wonders or disasters we are ourselves. We have no other models to go by. Frankenstein is my own reflection in the mirror. And it occurred to me that the mirror Marek stared at fifty years ago might have been the primeval soup I had read about, the forbidding swamp we had been talking about.

Three-Three

A frenzy of construction surrounded me as I stepped out of the bus near Bonifraterska. Earthmovers, bobcats, concrete mixers stood or scurried around wherever I looked. Diesel engines kept up a monotonous refrain, occasionally changing pitch as if trying to catch their breath. Metal clashed against metal, scraped against concrete and stone. Even the sky seemed to be littered with cranes and pile drivers for which there seemed no place on the ground. All this energy was strangely at odds with the laboured, lugubrious walking of older folk for some of whom these construction sites might have once been home. A strong wind blew dust into my eyes and my mouth as I walked along absent-mindedly.

Soon I found myself at one corner of a field where I had spent many afternoons just hanging around. I tried to imagine myself there - four, five years ago. However much I pride myself on my memory, this exercise proved more difficult than I had bargained for. Entire episodes from my life seemed blanked out, censored by some new regime, others glossed to the point where they were unrecognizable. I knew I might have to wait a long time for Stan to turn up. So I had brought along Martin's story, the one Tetsuo had woken me up with that morning.

* * *

SAMMY AND THE KING OF KIKBUTZ

I

The King of Kikbutz ruled over a land that was vast, beautiful, and rich. He belonged to the PuPuan race, a

142

tall, handsome community of men and women, much admired - even envied - by other less important races who also lived in and around Kikbutz. The largest and poorest of the other races was the Darkuns. As a young man, the King considered himself a compassionate human being. Touched by the Darkuns' plight, he decided to do something. In a fit of generosity, he made up his mind to do the Darkuns a favour. So, the day he became king he vowed that his kingdom would be a place of kindness, of gentleness. He thought for a long time and asked: "What could be softer, gentler than candle-light?" "Nothing" came the resounding answer from his ministers. From that day onwards, the King ordered his subjects to light thousands of candles each night. It was a beautiful sight at first, each glowing flame a symbol of hope.

The PuPuans were a proud people. But they professed unanimously that they were not proud of their good looks. It was their minds, their brains, that they were proudest of. They thought of their minds as neat little machines perfected over hundreds, even thousands, of years. Their neat little brains had helped the PuPuans develop the most marvellous gadgets that left them free to play, make love, and imagine their world to be a latter day Garden of Eden.

Other races like the Darkuns had minds that were less than perfect. Some eminent scientists theorized that it was because their brains were smaller than those of the PuPuans. The Darkuns certainly found it difficult to stand up to the PuPuans. Unchallenged and free to impose their will on others, the PuPuans thought of themselves as gentle and peace-loving. They applauded the King's brilliant idea.

Kings usually have everything they could ever want. But if there was one thing the King of Kikbutz craved, it was greatness. "I want to be remembered," he was fond of telling the Queen. He wanted to be remembered for greatness, and his single-minded pursuit of this quality seemed to lead naturally to power. Each day, wrapped in a gossamer cloak of peace, the King of Kikbutz appeared more and more invincible. Born to greatness, toughened in battles fought in his youth, with an intellect honed in the finest seats of learning, Destiny had opened before his eyes the innermost secrets of emperors, charlatans, and even the most ordinary of mortals. Or so he was convinced. Lesser mortals smiled and scraped in his presence, but feared him like the plague at other times.

II

Sammy, the little black boy, lived only a stone's throw away from the palace walls. He did not fear the King, but his life was full of fear just the same. The King was smart enough to know of the plight of little children like Sammy who belonged to the Darkuns and other inferior races. And had the King not pledged to protect the interest of every single human being? Yes, he had to think of everyone, even the lowliest of those who helped put together the fearsome PuPu kites, and the smartest of those who gathered and doled out the wealth that made everything possible. As a matter of fact, one of the King's decrees forbade PuPuans to call any race inferior. Nobody questioned the decree, but the proud PuPuans knew of their ordained place at the top with an unshakeable certainty.

Thanks to the uncounted wealth of Kikbutz and their fearsome PuPu kites, these were heady times. The world was changing at a dizzying pace. For starters, The Wall was gone. It had been such a terrible menace. For years, people raged against it from both sides. Nothing happened. So people learned - or felt compelled - to live with it, in a grudging sort of way. A dark and forbidding wall it was, stretching for miles, slicing through the heart of a beautiful city, making prisoners of those on the inside and aliens of those on the other. At the foot of the wall, every year there sprouted a few more crosses remembering those who had tried to cross the wall and failed. Flowers, fresh, dead, and dying, lay strewn among the crosses, left there by strangers. They said that on quiet, moonless nights, when the wind was still, you could sit under the walls and listen to the spirits singing sad melodies of lost love. But not for long. The patrolling armoured vehicles were sure to move in, shine their blinding lights on you, and call on you through their bull-horns to move on.

Sammy and the King of Kikbutz lived on the same side of the wall, the good side. So, when the King of Kikbutz claimed credit, in a modest sort of way, for dismantling The Wall, for changing the face of the earth as it were, a wave of excitement swept through the land. Sammy heard the King and his heart filled with hope. Sammy hadn't eaten a decent meal in months, but he was convinced better times were around the corner. Sammy cared little about the wall. From morning till night, all he knew was hunger.

III

To many, it now seemed the springtime of a new age. The King had fooled Igor, the Eastern potentate, into stepping down from his throne. Not only that, Igor found that his entire kingdom had vanished into thin air and pretty soon he was beginning to be remembered as the Prince of the Vanishing Country. "We have prevailed," chuckled the King of Kikbutz, "as I had promised my people we would." Closer to home, Norris, a tin-pot dope peddling dictator, was bound in chains and hauled back to Kikbutz by a victorious army. But nothing changed for Sammy. Hope settled back into quiet despair.

"Mother," he cried, "I am hungry." But his mother could only look back helplessly at him. One day, when he found his hunger overpowering, Sammy simply walked out of a crowded supermarket with a loaf of bread in his hand and a half dozen cans of Spam and tuna stuffed in his pockets.

"Right on," exclaimed his sister Paula, young and pretty, the envy of all the neighbourhood girls and the spark of every man's arousal. "I'll take care of my tricks," she said, "you just take care of supper." Their mother simply cried.

During the day, they sat transfixed before the TV screen and heard people say that the human race was waking up from a terrible dream. Sometimes the speakers sounded even more profound and said that the dream was perhaps all too real. It was sad enough, they said, that the wall had cut a swath through the city. What was sadder still was that it meandered through vast countries and the endless countryside and entered people's hearts. The soothsayers were divided on how long it would take to bring it all down. All this made little sense to Sammy, but he sat through it all with his mother and sister just the same.

The soothsayers, otherwise known as pollsters, determined that most people believed the nightmare was over. It certainly seemed so when, in a dazzling display of magical arms, the Kizhands were vanquished, thousands upon thousands of their warriors turned into pillars of ash for having dared to covet a land they considered worse than Sodom, more despicable than Gomorrah. And of course the mighty Wall already lay in ruins, its chunks of concrete hauled away as souvenirs. Behind the Wall a vast kingdom stirred from years of being lulled by fear they had mistaken for freedom, lulled by laws of science painted with the stirring hues of religion. As the Wall fell to pieces, and the gusts circled the burning desert, fierce winds blew through the gaping holes and scattered the truths that had mesmerized the people for nearly a hundred years. A melancholy restlessness seized the people now, even PuPuans now unprotected by the Wall.

Then came sickness, for as the wind blew over the land it unleashed a terrible disease. One that stung the flesh and numbed the mind. When the panic subsided, people imagined that, like everything else, this too would pass. Gradually, folks got used to this too and learned to live with it. Then came the next wave. This time, the virus went straight for the heart, sparing not even those who were strong, healthy, and rich.

"Seems like a punishment from God," said the King of Kikbutz thoughtfully.

"And well deserved," echoed his priests.

To most PuPuans, the sickness seemed at first like the bite of a pesky bug, a minor irritation at worst. So the celebration, the festivities, continued. The land was decked out in colour. Parades with marching bands clogged the streets in cities and towns. "A world divided in two is now blessed with a single, pre-eminent power," said the King of Kikbutz. "Rejoice." The King of Kikbutz knew his testaments, old and new, and was quick to recognize the changes around him as changes of biblical proportions. "By the strength of arms," he said, "we laid waste the heathens in the desert." He added, "And by the grace of God we have won the other war."

"Praise be to the all merciful God," droned his priests and courtiers.

"The messengers of Darkness fly in disarray and terror," continued the King. "What a wondrous breed of PuPuans we sent into the desert. They've made us so proud." Later, in a moving speech to his people from the palace, the King proclaimed, "Let us look homeward now. Let us set right what needs to be set right."

Didn't some folks say the problem wasn't in the wall really, but in people's hearts? Sammy's mother thought so. Others disagreed. They pointed to the inferior races as lazy, lumps of clod, baby machines at best. "Make wealth, not babies," became the watchword of the new age.

In spite of it all, it became harder and harder to find food. But the lights seemed to help, the thousands of candles lit by royal decree. For when the rich slept in their beds, the Darkuns were out searching for food in alleys and side-streets. Many found their meals in trash-cans.

IV

The days started to grow shorter, and Sammy's mother always found herself cold. She liked to make a joke of it by placing her hands unexpectedly against Sammy's face. She said, "An icy hand, much colder than this, has curled itself around peoples' hearts and frozen such feelings as kindness and mercy." As a little boy, Sammy never quite understood what his mother was talking about. He was just as bewildered when, on her deathbed, she said, "It's like a sore, that's what grows in the place of love."

Sammy no longer cried for food. Paula had moved in with Spikey, and Sammy's mother was reduced to selling her body for food. It was a losing battle. Her body swelled up with life again and again, and all she could do was pluck the fruit from out of her womb. She grew weaker each day, and the family seemed to need more food than ever before. Soon, there was little of his mother's body to sell. One day, the dreaded wind trapped her in its spell. Sammy's mother caught the terrible sickness, one that seemed to open the floodgates to every other disease. She wasted away and died quietly on a summer's day. There were no flowers for Sammy's mother. No one seemed to notice. No one seemed to care.

Little by little, Sammy began to understand. Millions of children went hungry, but billions went to pay for shining weapons that drew the envy and admiration of all who lacked and wanted them. So when Spikey asked him to run with packets of white powder from one apartment to the other, one car to the other, and paid him very well for it, Sammy began to see what destiny held in store for him. Spikey carried a gun inside his vest and people feared and respected him. "Let them police the skies," said Spikey, "we're happy with the street." But alone after his mother's death, Sammy soon lost interest in this line of work.

V

Even as the King grew in his power, prosperity seemed to be slipping away from the land of Kikbutz. "Can there be others," wondered the King, "as blessed as we are?" Every other inconsequential kingdom seemed to be in trouble, except a solitary island crammed with short, strange people. "We will watch them," he said, "and we will prevail."

Indeed, nothing escaped the King. In the borders of the desert lived a skulking thing of no consequence - a fart, as far as the King of Kikbutz was concerned. But the King watched him like a hawk, for he had unseen eyes in the sky. One day, his advisers brought him news that the inconsequential fart had crashed his flying machine in the desert. The eyes had seen it all.

"Good riddance," said the King.

"Amen," echoed his minions.

But the thing of no consequence lived. And this raised two important theological questions. Either there was a heathen god not wholly impotent, or that the true God let his mercy fall on believers and heathens alike. The latter possibility was somewhat disturbing and the King decided it warranted closer scrutiny. He would scatter a few pieces of silver before some stuffy academics and let them fry their brains in futile debate. That would be fun.

One day, as he stood on the shores of his summer palace, the King thought he heard a voice rising above the waves crashing at his feet. It was the sea speaking to him.

"O great King of Kikbutz," said the ocean, "your people call you a wimp."

"My forefathers came to this land and drove off the savages through the might of arms," replied the King angrily. "Who calls me a wimp? I'll show my people the stuff I'm made of."

The King held his ear to the wind a long time but heard nothing more. "I know who thinks me a wimp," he said, "who else but the Darkuns. The enemy grows in my shadow."

With great difficulty, the King brought his anger under control, for 'anger' - like many other four and five-letter words - was a dirty word in Kikbutz. Like other PuPuans, the King was expected to react with power and determination, but not in anger.

Outsiders are often surprised to know that one of the most respected words in Kikbutz is 'poop'. Poops were those people who held real power in Kikbutz. They occupied positions in the Senate, in the Congress, and controlled all administrative functions like the police, the army, and sanitation services. Well, it was the Council of Poops that the King now called to his summer palace.

"I want some changes in the land," said the King to his Council. "As of tonight, no more candles."

The Councillors looked puzzled. The Chief Councillor said, "Have you not noticed, O King, that the candles no longer burn at night?"

"What?" asked the King.

"Perhaps it has something to do with the disease that's sweeping through the land," continued the Chief Councillor. "Each day, more and more of our men and women grow sharp beaks upon their mouths. What's worse is that their fingers and toes are starting to curl inwards like talons. Makes it very difficult to strike matches and light fires. Over the past few months, as the disease has spread, so has the number of lights grown less and less."

"I can believe that," said the King. "Some of you guys are starting to look pretty awful." He looked thoughtfully from one councillor's face to the other. "So all the lights are out?" he finally asked.

"No, great Lord," said another Councillor, "we have seen one candle, one single light, that seems to burn each night."

"Find it and put it out," ordered the King as he dismissed the men. "Remember," he called after them, "the only lights in the kingdom will be those that we choose to light."

As the lights went out in Kikbutz, people, mostly the inferior races searching for scraps, began to think up all kinds of clever schemes to share and spread whatever light there still remained. When the Councillors discovered that people were using mirrors to reflect the light from kitchen fires, wood fires, even cigarette lighters, especially at night, they decided something needed to be done.

The Council of Poops finally took an ingenious plan to their King. "Let us destroy all mirrors in the land," they said.

"Our orders must be carried out," said the King sternly. "We must prevail. Let the mirrors be destroyed."

The Chief Councillor came up with another brilliant idea. "Let us destroy the mirrors at night," he said. "They'll be less upset when they're asleep."

That night, the sound of shattering glass roused many people from their sleep. But since they couldn't see what was happening, almost everyone went back to bed or simply remained there, listening. Still, as the King looked out of his palace window in the wee hours of the morning, he thought he saw one single light in the distance. He couldn't sleep any more that night.

The next morning, an angry King called the Council of Poops and demanded an explanation for the one light he had seen the night before.

"Great King," spoke the Chief Councillor nervously, "it has become very difficult to spot who holds the one lighted candle we see from time to time. The kingdom is too dark at night. But we've seen it so often near trash cans and dumpsters that we suspect it's someone scavenging for food."

"That's strange," said the King. "I thought we had banished hunger from the land."

"We had come pretty close, O King!" said another Councillor, "until we went to war with the Kizhands. We used up so much of our food in arming our Poopoo Kites that we now have a serious problem. Also, because we won the war so handsomely, every country on earth wants our poop."

"But they can't have it, can they?" asked the King.

"Not according to the law," replied the Chief Councillor. "But the truth is all the food in the country seems to be going to the Poopooo Kite factories."

"Ah well," said the King thoughtfully, "at least we have our pride. Citizens of Kikbutz can walk tall once more. We have finally buried the ghost of our last defeat in the Battle of Scorched Rats fifteen years ago."

"Yes, O King!" cried the Council of Poops in unison, "they're all singing your praise in the streets."

"Sing it again, Poops," said the King. "It is sweet music to my ears."

And the Councillors sang:

Your guiding light, your wisdom
Brought the Kizhands down, O King.
Of all the weapons the earth has seen
The Poopoo Kite's the thing.

King Subman of the Kizhands
He had them Kites as well;
What he didn't have was expertise
That sends young men to hell.

Our scientists worked all day and night
Until they had the scoop.
They stirred and squeezed new
Formulae to concentrate the poop.

It's not the size of Poopoo Kites
That snuffed their evil lies,
But the load of poop that fell
Like vengeance from the skies.

As the Councillors sang, they noticed a change
come over their King. Slowly but surely, it seemed the
disease was starting to take hold of him. The King's
face was beginning to grow a fearsome beak much like
an eagle's.

The song ended, and the King clapped his hands
in delight. He had every reason to be proud. He had
vowed to change the face of the earth, and he had. He
had decreed that non-PuPuans would never again be
allowed to fly kites. Wars would disappear forever.
Who would dare break the peace as long as PuPuans
had their kites?

VI

And so the days passed by. The King's face had now turned grey and drawn, almost as ugly as those of his Councillors. But, with all the mirrors smashed throughout the land, the King couldn't tell what was happening to him. Certainly, his Councillors weren't telling. And the Queen didn't wish to break his heart.

Each evening, the King would head out from his palace for long walks along the coast. One day, he got tired of walking. He sat down on the sand for a long time until the evening grew dark. "Tell me, Sea," he asked, "do my people still think of me a wimp?"

This time, the sea said nothing. The King heard no voices, only the sound of laughter. He began to feel lonely and wished the candlelights of his early days as King would drive the darkness away.

As if in answer to his wishes, a single point of light appeared in the distance. It drew closer and closer until the King saw a little Darkun boy holding a candle, walking along the sand. It was Sammy.

The boy was almost in front of him now. The King stretched his arms and reached out towards the boy. It was then he realized that his fingers were no more. They had all turned into sharp, angry claws.

The King of Kikbutz dropped his hands in horror and despair. Little Sammy walked past him and soon became invisible in the night.

* * * * *

I sat back against the park bench and closed my eyes against the wind, wondering what to make of my father's story. A fable of sorts? Martin Fisher's reflections on the Gulf War he had seen in Iraq? I also tried to put the story in the context of Martin's cryptic note which Tetsuo had given me. The sun seeped warmly through my shirt and began to weigh down my eyelids with sleep. I shook myself awake as my head jerked back to the limits of my neck. I had not prepared myself for the shock. Standing in front of me, dressed impeccably, a cigarette dangling from a corner of his mouth, a beret holding his golden hair in place, was Stan. I seemed to have lost my voice just then.

"Which is it?" he asked slyly. "Misha or Matthew?"

I remained silent, for I honestly didn't know.

"Surprised?" he asked again.

It almost seemed as though we had met in a different life, in a different world. "I sure am," I confessed. "When did you get out?"

Stan blew some smoke into the air then crushed the flaming tip under his heels. "Quite some time ago."

"Really?" I asked, somewhat incredulous, trying to put his answer in the web of my own four years in prison.

He smiled and sat down next to me. "I know it's hard to stomach after your own sentence," he said. "We have the kind of power even grown-ups don't have. What do you call it?" He turned to look at me. "Ah!" he came up immediately with the answer. "Immunity," adding quickly, "and a good lawyer."

"I thought I had a damn good lawyer."

Stan adjusted his beret and shook his hair in the process. "You also need good connections," he reminded me.

In the eyes of the law, sixteen was something of a magic number. At the time of Olga's death, I was on the wrong side of sixteen, and not even my most heartfelt incantations of *Adair Adair* could help me overpower that magic. We sat quietly. There seemed little to talk about. Finally, he broke the silence. "I'm sorry for what happened to Olga. I truly am." I couldn't find anything to say in response, so we continued to sit in silence. I felt no anger, no hostility. I felt nothing towards Stan. He offered me a cigarette.

"I've got to go," I said, looking at my watch.

"May I join you?" he asked.

The question stopped me dead in my tracks. I didn't know what to say. Finally, I managed to blurt out, "I'm going to Marek's for a reading of something he has written."

Stan's eyes lit up at my words. "Please let me come," he said softly. "Perhaps Marek won't mind too much, or he can throw me out. I know Jews detest us Gypsies."

"As much as you detest them?" I couldn't resist asking.

Stan closed his eyes, shrugged his shoulder, and said nothing. I didn't tell him Marek was dead. I couldn't. I don't know what I was waiting for. Stan had appeared like a bridge to another world, another life. That world was peopled with those I loved deeply. And they were still there as if nothing had changed. Stan had been late in coming, and that had given me time to finish reading Martin's story. What was he trying to tell us? That he was human, that he had a soul, feelings?

"Please," Stan interrupted my thoughts.

What could I say? I was hoping Connie and Tetsuo would show up around six. So it was shortly before six o'clock that we entered Marek's apartment. Connie was already there.

Not unexpectedly, a sudden chill descended on us all as she recognized Stan. But he had come with me, and Connie had no words to express her displeasure. Tetsuo, when he showed up, asked with obvious distaste, "What're you doing here?"

A sad smile was Stan's only answer. The pale lights came on as before as we began to settle down for the evening. And then the unexpected happened. I saw them walking in, the invited and the uninvited. Lydia came, looking sad and ill. Even Marek marched in though the open door, shouting greetings to us, trying to revive something of our ebbing conviviality. Stan didn't say anything. Marek simply nodded his head in acknowledgement of our presence. But Olga wasn't there, and I think I know why. I should have been less forgiving of Stan. But then, it seems inconceivable that the murderer and the victim face each other after a life is taken. A murderer would need to dream a victim back to life. Stan, through no fault of his, seemed incapable of dreams.

A wonderful aroma of strong coffee greeted us. I was glad for that because it overpowered every other smell that I knew from before. "Help yourself to coffee and anything else you want," said Connie.

Lydia had turned pale and exhausted walking up the stairs. I held her gently and led her to the most comfortable chair. Tetsuo started looking around for an electrical outlet, found one, and decided that the dining table would be okay to set up his portable sound system.

"That's neat. How much would a box like that cost?" asked Stan, admiring the stereo. "Could I borrow it sometime?"

"Not really," answered Tetsuo. "It belongs to the company."

"That means its yours," said Stan cheerfully. "You're the boss, aren't you?"

Tetsuo didn't answer. He busied himself setting the system in order. Marek's face was turned in the direction of Stan's voice. I could see he was trying to make out who it was, but he wasn't going to be drawn into any conversation with him.

"It's my friend, Stan, Marek," I finally said. The words almost stuck in my throat. "He wanted to come to the reading. You do remember Stan, Don't you?"

"How could I ever forget Stan. Well, make yourselves comfortable."

The others looked strangely at me. "Mumbling to yourself?" asked Connie.

I pretended I hadn't heard her. Gradually we eased ourselves into our chairs and glanced uncertainly at each other's faces. Lydia sat with her eyes closed, so I got up to fetch her a glass of water. Stan decided to look around the place. He walked from window to window and stopped in front of a cupboard where, carefully separated from a half dozen wine glasses, there stood a number of dolls wearing traditional dresses from different Polish regions.

I think Marek was ready for us, except that he hadn't been expecting Stan. When I told him there were five of us, including Stan, he seemed to be taken aback for a moment. His face hardened, and I was afraid he would ask me to lead him out of the apartment. Worried at finding me speaking - to myself, as it appeared to them - Connie and Tetsuo looked at me inquiringly. Stan was engrossed in the dolls and seemed totally out of it.

Marek recovered his composure soon enough. "I'm sorry I have written out only four of these invitations," he said, waving a bunch of papers in his hand. "Would you pass them around please, Misha," he said to me. "Maybe Stan could read yours if he wanted to."

The piece of paper seemed to contain some sort of an invitation. Stan was looking over Lydia's shoulder, since she seemed to be holding it in her hand but not reading it. "Today isn't the 15th of July," he remarked, starting to walk back to the cupboard of the dolls.

"Every day is the 15th of July," retorted Marek, a touch of mockery in his voice.

Stan stopped in his tracks. At the same time he caught sight of Lydia lifting up the piece of paper for him. He took the paper from her hand. "Thank you," he said softly, adding, "Are you not feeling well?" She nodded her head to say no.

"Can I get myself a beer?" asked Stan, turning away from Lydia.

"Of course you can," I said. "Connie had me bring in a bunch only yesterday." I pointed Stan in the direction of the fridge.

"I had a role for you, Lydia," whispered Marek. "Actually, it was a role I had written with Olga in mind. But it seems to have vanished. All my papers, the entire file, seems to have disappeared. But never mind. My memory is as good as it was fifty years ago."

Lydia smiled weakly. So she could hear Marek, could she? She seemed relieved she didn't have to read any voices. She looked terribly sick, and my heart went out to her. I wanted to be close to her, to hold her in my arms like before.

Connie hadn't said much since we had come. She now looked strangely tense and distraught, and I wondered if she had had a fight with Tetsuo. She must have seen me look questioningly at her, for she asked, "Would you like us to put on the music?"

At the sound of her voice I looked more closely at her and was relieved to find her looking much more relaxed than earlier in the afternoon.

"I know Marek is dead," Stan suddenly said, "and so is Lydia."

Just then, I hated Stan for having shattered my spell, one which seemed to have brought us all together. "Damn you," I murmured in desperation.

Lydia was the first to disappear. But Marek stayed a while. "This wasn't the way it was supposed to have ended," he said. "You were to have been the flower girl who brought blossoms for Amal, for Abrasha, for all of us. Now we must cover you with flowers." With that, Marek was gone as well.

If Martin Fisher hadn't shown up in my dream that evening, there probably was a good reason. Only recently, during one of his last visits to me in prison, quite out of the blue Martin Fisher said to me, "I'm going home to your mother."

I wasn't sure if I had heard him right. My first impulse was to think of Lydia. But Lydia was dead. What was this man talking about? I looked up at him quickly. Tough jaws set over a powerful neck, his unswerving eyes looking straight ahead, his lean body well browned under the sun. No, there was nothing to suggest the man might be out of his mind. "Say that again," I asked.

"I'm going back to your mother," he repeated.

"You can't be serious."

"I am," he said, never moving for a moment his eyes that seemed set on something in front of him. "And I would like you to come with me." There was a pause which I needed badly to let the words sink in. "And I very much hope you will come."

I couldn't find any words in response. Was this a lifebelt he was tossing out to his drowning son? How was he to know the turmoil and uncertainty that I was in just then? And I remembered the future as a black hole, an image I had thought about quite a lot of late. "My mother lives deep inside a black hole," I said. "You left her there many years ago and walked away. You let her sink into that hole until she was no longer even a memory. I can't even think of her as a person."

"Stop," he said, "you have no right to punish me." He was now looking straight at me. "That black hole is one no one can escape, neither you nor I. I saw your mother enter it back home. I have seen friends discover it in war, seen it open up in the wide ocean as the wind howled around our drilling rigs caught in a tempest. It opens up wherever, when you least expect it. I have been drawn into it and I didn't know it. I have been travelling through it in time. I passed Lydia along the way, and many others you've never met. They each had their journeys cut out for them. I must be about to bottom out, because as I get closer and closer to the end all I can see is your mother. I loved her once and loved her deeply until she could love me no more. Maybe it was the sight of the black hole that made her mad, while I pretended it didn't exist." My father's voice drifted into a whisper. "I should've been with her all along, holding her hand, walking together. I failed her. Like a fool I've been walking alone."

I couldn't bear to look at my father for the tears that welled up in my eyes. "It's the Post Office, isn't it?" I asked. "Marek was telling me the truth all along. Amal wants his letter. Amal wants to be the king's mailman. He must enter the post-office, and so must we. Suddenly, everything became so simple I wished I hadn't wasted my hours in prison. In the great scheme of things, what had Darwin to offer me that I couldn't find in Marek's songs.

It was my father's turn to question me. "The Post Office?" he asked.

"Yes, the play Marek had once seen and loved so much."

"I think Marek had seen much more, much much more," said my father. "I think he had seen me too," he continued softly, "years before he saw through me." For once, I found it so easy to agree with Martin Fisher.

Shortly afterwards, in the midst of my dejection and self-pity, and adding to my scepticism about people in general, I received a letter from mother. Never in my life had I received so much as a scribbled note from her. But now she was announcing a windfall. It was an invitation to a party in Calgary's ritzy Palliser Hotel celebrating a $100,000 settlement she had received from the provincial government. I was to discover still later that it was the government's way of saying sorry to fifty or so women who had been forcibly sterilized during an earlier, darker period of our history.

Could it be true, I asked myself, that there was something miraculous about my birth? My peculiar skin condition had often made me wonder if the marks were something in the nature of stigmata. The evidence of people such as Stephen Langton of Canterbury and Saint Francis of Assisi didn't seem to match my own. These folk and many others experienced wounds in their hands and feet with actual nails appearing in their wounds. My hands and feet were fine, and there were certainly no nails in my body.

One day, quite by chance, I came across the story of Elizabeth, a thirteenth century nun, who claimed she had seen Christ's crucifixion. She found stigmata on her forehead like those caused by Christ's crown of thorns. It occurred to me that the Star of David, symbolically speaking, might not be that different from a crown of thorns. But to add any credibility to this conjecture, I had to be certain about my birth. Only Martin Fisher could confirm the details, whether or not mine was of the miraculous kind. But now he had gone home.

This evening, I noticed for the first time that the apartment was in terrible shape. Brown coffee stains stared down at us, possibly from bathroom leakages in the floors above. The plaster had fallen off from several points in the ceiling. The wallpaper was peeling. It was hard to imagine how cheerfully Marek lived through it all. The music was wailing softly. "Let's see where we were yesterday?" asked Tetsuo.

"Amal is at the window, talking to the boys outside," replied Connie.

Tonight, the wind was silent, and the spirits invisible.

* * * * *

[Enter Madhav]

Madhav: *Go away, go away, you irksome kids. We don't want you crowding around this window. Can't you see Amal is ill?*

Amal: *Must I leave the window too? I really feel fine, I do. If I leave now, I fear my Fakir will pass by and miss visiting with me.*

Madhav: *That's strange. I don't know of any Fakirs.*

[Enter Fakir]

Well, I'll be damned.

Amal: *Where have you been this time, Fakir?*

Fakir: *To the Isle of Parrots. You see, I'm not like you. A journey doesn't cost me a cent. I go just wherever I please.*

Amal: *But you promised to teach me your magic. Please do, so I can fly away to the Isle of Parrots.*

Madhav: *Magic? What nonsense! What're you talking about?*

Amal: *I promise I won't leave until I'm well. But, Fakir, tell me what sort of a place is it, this Isle of Parrots?*

Fakir: *Ah! the green island is like an emerald set in the deep blue sea. And when the parrots fly away in the morning it seems the emerald is shattering into pieces. Come evening, and the pieces come together once again. Peace returns as the ocean rocks the island to sleep.*

Amal: *How beautiful. I wish I was a parrot.*

Fakir: *But the Milkman said you were planning to be a curd seller.*

Madhav: *Oh! I forgot to tell you. The Milkman has left you a bowl of curd. He couldn't wait because he had to go to his niece's wedding.*

Amal: *How odd! the Milkman told me he's going to marry me to his little niece. She would be*

my lovely bride with a pair of pearl drops in
her ears, all dressed in red and gold. Every
morning she would milk with her own hands
the black cow and bring me warm milk with
foam on it in an earthen cup. And in the eve-
ning, she would first carry the lamp round
the barn and the house to ward off evil spirits,
and then come sit by me and tell me stories of
Champa and her seven brothers.

Fakir: *Don't worry, even if she's gone, I can still find*
          you many more pretty nieces.

Madhav: *This is too much. I can't take it any more.*

                                        [Exit Madhav]

"Would you mind very much if I exited too?" Stan interrupted at this point. "I'm hungry."

"Help yourself," Connie told him, trying to hide her impa-
tience. "There's eggs, bread, milk, cereal, and not much else.
All in the kitchen."

"Great," answered Stan, as he stood up and walked into
the kitchen. "Better not ruin Tetsuo's music with the sound
of eggs frying," he said, looking back at us with a broad smile
that made him appear as strong as he was beautiful. With
that, he shut the kitchen door behind him. Connie looked at
me with a knowing smile and rolled her eyes heavenwards.
Then we continued.

Amal: *Fakir, now that Uncle has left, tell me, has the*
          King sent me a letter to the post-office?

Fakir: *I gather the letter has left his desk. It's on its*
          way here.

Amal: *On its way? Where is it? Is it somewhere on that winding road through the trees, the one you follow to the end of the forest on a clear day? Yes, I can see it all. There, the King's postman coming down the moss-laden hillside alone, a lantern in his left hand, a bag of letters on his back. He has been climbing down for ever so long, days and nights. He has to reach the foot of the mountain where the waterfall becomes a river. There he washes his feet on the bank and walks through the ripening rye. Now comes the sugar-cane field and he disappears into the narrow lane hacked through the sugar-cane stems. I can see it so clearly. He reaches the open meadow where the cricket chirps and there's not a single person to be seen, only the snipe wagging their tail and poking into the mud with their bills. I am so glad now that I can feel him drawing nearer and nearer . . . . . Fakir, do you personally know this King who has this new post office?*

Fakir: *I do. I go to him to beg for alms every day.*

Amal: *When I get well, I must have my alms from him too. I'll go to his gate and say, "Make me your postman that I may go about, lantern in hand, passing out your letters from door to door. Oh! please don't let me stay at home all day." . . . . . Fakir, there's a beggar who has promised to teach me how to beg.*

Fakir: *Which one is that?*

Amal: *The blind cripple who's pushed around in a box with wheels by a boy much like me. I've promised to wheel him around when I'm better. Uncle won't give him alms. Thinks he's faking his blindness.*

Fakir: *Why does he come to your window, if he doesn't get any alms.*

Amal: *Because I tell him stories. I tell him everything you and the others tell me. Remember the story of the land where everything is light as a feather, where you can fly over mountains and streams without even trying. He loved the story, and now he wants to know how to get there.*

Fakir: *It is possible.*

Amal: *I doubt if he'll ever make it though. He's blind, you see. Poor man, he just has to keep on begging. But at least he has someone to wheel him around.*

Fakir: *You hate it in here, don't you?*

Amal: *In the beginning there was nothing to do. But now, the very sight of the King's post office makes me happy. Once there was only an open field. Now there's a roof, and walls, and a gate. I'm just happy sitting here, waiting for the letter that I know will come. I wonder what the King's message will be.*

Fakir: *What really matters is your name on the letter.*

[Enter Madhav]

Suddenly, Tetsuo asked, "I'm sorry to interrupt, but do you smell something?"

I felt somewhat slighted. "I always smell something around here," I replied without thinking. "I don't smell anything different."

Maybe Stan was frying eggs. We returned to our play. The music played on. I kept on dreaming of Amal, wishing the dream wouldn't end. Connie had just started to speak her lines when Tetsuo interrupted. She continued.

Madhav: *The two of you have got me into a real pickle. The Headman has written to the King that we imagine ourselves above our humble station in life. We're supposed to be talking about messages from Kings all the time.*

Amal: *Is the King angry?*

Fakir: *The King has more important things to worry about.*

Amal: *Say, Fakir, I've been feeling a kind of darkness coming over my eyes since the morning. Everything's wrapped in a haze, like a dream. I must be quiet. I don't feel like talking any more. Won't the King's letter come? Suppose this room melts away all of a sudden, just suppose. . . .*

Fakir: *The letter's sure to come today.*

[Enter Physician]

Physician: *And how do you feel today, young man?*

Amal: *Feel awfully good today. All the pain seems to have gone.*

Physician: *There's something strange in the air. As I came in, I found a fearful draught blowing through your front door. That's most hurtful. Better shut the door at once. Would it matter if you kept your visitors away for two or three days? If someone happens to call unexpectedly, there's always the back door. You had better shut the windows as well. The rays of the setting sun will only keep the child awake.*

[Enter Headman]

Headman: *Hello! you little brat.*

Fakir: *You must be quiet.*

Amal: *No, no, Fakir. Did you think I was asleep? I wasn't. I can hear everything. I can hear voices far away.*

Headman: *Don't you see why the King plants his post-office right before your window? Why, you little brat, there's a letter for you from the King.*

Amal: *Oh, really?*

Headman: *How can it not be true? You're the King's pal. Here's your letter.* [Showing a blank slip of paper] *Ha! ha! ha! This is the letter.*

Amal: *Please don't mock me. Say, Fakir, is it so?*

Fakir: *Yes, I as Fakir tell you it is his letter.*

Amal: *How is it I can't see? It all looks so blank to me. What is there in the letter, Mr. Headman?*

Headman: *The King says, "I'm calling on you shortly. Make sure you have some puffed rice for me.*

	I find the palace food quite tasteless these days. Ha! ha! ha!
Amal:	*Fakir, Fakir. Shh! his trumpet. Can't you hear?*
Headman:	*Ha! ha! I fear he won't rest until he's a bit more off his head.*
Amal:	*You bring me such joy. Let me seek your blessings. Let me wipe the dust off your feet.*
Headman:	*The little child does have an instinct for reverence. Though a little silly, he has a good heart.*
Amal:	*Is the evening star up yet? How come I can't see it?*

[Λ loud knocking outside]

Madhav:	*They've smashed the outer door.*

[The King's Herald enters]

Herald:	*Our Sovereign King comes tonight.*
Amal:	*At what hour of the night, Herald?*
Herald:	*On the second watch . . . . . The King sends his greatest physician to attend on his young friend.*

[Enter State Physician]

Physician:	*What's this? Everything's shut up in here. Open wide all the doors and windows.*
Amal:	*All the pain is gone. I can see the stars burning through the night's curtain of darkness.*
Physician:	*Will you be well enough to leave your bed? The King comes in the middle watches of the night.*

Madhav: *My child, the King loves you. He is coming himself. Do beg for a small gift from him. You know how humble and poor we are.*

Amal: *I shall ask him for all I've ever wanted. I'll ask him to make me one of his postmen so I may roam far and wide, delivering his message from door to door.*

Physician: *Now be quiet, all of you. Sleep is coming over him. I'll sit by his pillow. He's dropping off to sleep. Hush, he sleeps.*

    [Sudha enters]

Sudha: *I have some flowers for Amal. May I not place them in his own hands.*

Physician: *Yes, you may.*

Sudha: *When will he be awake?*

Physician: *As soon as the King comes and calls him.*

Sudha: *Will you whisper a word or two from me, in his ear?*

Physician: *What shall I say?*

Sudha: *Tell him Sudha has not forgotten him.*

* * * * *

The play had ended, but the music played on, blending its harmony with the music in my head. I could feel their presence - Marek, Lydia, even Martin. It was as if they were all part of Korczak's audience, on Chlodna Street, audience and players all woven into a tapestry of memories. Tetsuo, self-effacing as ever, flooded our lives with music, the music of others, which he made ours to keep forever.

Our peace and harmony were soon shattered. There was a strange sound like a chair crashing to the floor in the next room. "You okay, Stan?" Connie called out. There was no answer. After a while Connie got up. "I need a glass of water," she said, walking to the kitchen.

"Oh! Stan," screamed Connie as, wild-eyed, she ran out of the kitchen and gestured for us to walk back in.

A chair lay upturned on the floor. Hanging from a hook in the ceiling was Stan, his neck broken, his open mouth moist with froth. Tetsuo ran to right the chair, then climbed on it to free Stan's body from the choking leather belt. I stared uncomprehendingly at Stan lying on the floor, his head resting on a pillow someone had fetched from the bed. It seemed he had gone to sleep, which he had, dressed in all his finery. The lower edges of his brown leather vest skimmed the floor. The leather patch on his Levi's glared straight at my face from one side of his body. And then I noticed he was wearing a pair of brand new Adidas. I couldn't help remembering my own craving for such a pair, and felt surprised over how and when the craving had suddenly disappeared. And my Bluejays cap. I simply couldn't remember what I had done with it.

The crowd watched as the stretcher, covered with sheets and strapped from side to side, was lifted into the ambulance. Those who had apartments in the front of Marek's building and in the building opposite to his looked down from behind curtains and windows at the street below. Others less fortunate with a discreet view of the events gathered on the opposite sidewalk. They remained silent, uncertain about what to make of it all.

This was the second time in less than two weeks that they had witnessed such a scene. The neighbourhood was falling apart. The ambulance switched on its siren and roared away in a cloud of blue smoke. The two police cars followed. So it was that Marck and Stan went their separate ways. Maybe they were travelling the same road, Stan to mail his apology to Marek at the post office, Marek to collect his mail. And Martin's manuscript. I decided to burn it.

October 14, 1998

A balding, fatherly police officer offered to take Connie home. Sick and exhausted, she finally left for her apartment around midnight. She would return early in the morning, she promised. Tetsuo stared out of the window all night long as he played Gorecki over and over again. A sensation of living in a less than real world descended on us. The future lay locked outside of Marek's door. Only the present, in which we felt trapped, seemed real. I too stayed up all night rummaging through the remainder of Marek's belongings.

As Tetsuo stood against the window, his white shirt draped over wide shoulders and a lean body, his rich mop of jet black hair one with the darkness behind him, I half expected him to turn with a baton in one hand and, with a flick of his wrist, start the music all over again. I hoped he and Connie might get together again. They had given me what I had always craved - unconditional friendship.

There was soon to be a spectacular sunrise that morning, something quite unusual for Warsaw. It made me wish I was back home once again - back home, younger, carefree and foolish.

This was to be the last day of my parole. As dawn touched the clouds above with delicate brush strokes of red, it awakened me to the other unreality that awaited me the next morning. Somehow, I needed to gather my energy to link the past into the future, to arrive at a coherent meaning of life, and an accurate understanding of who I was. Where had I come from? What was the real secret of my birth? When was my mother, if she was truly my mother, sterilized? Did life really begin from the primeval ooze - some of which lay frozen in the shales of Burgess Ridge - the ooze to which we will eventually disintegrate in the oven and in the grave.

Where were we for two billion years while the ooze sputtered and threw up the fossils that so convinced Martin Fisher of the origins of life in the Burgess Ridge. The exciting life we passed on our treks - the snow-shoe hare poking through white heather and wintergreen, the squirrel and porcupine swishing past meadows of red paintbrush, the black bear and elk pausing majestically over carpets of yellow poppies and buttercup - did they really owe their existence to the odd fossil shapes locked in the shale? Could it be that Martin knew something others didn't? Yet, in retrospect, he seemed so pedestrian that I feel reluctant to grant him any special knowledge.

These thoughts make me feel odd, make me look odd in the eyes of others. Would I remain impregnable against the assaults of the millennium bug? I can see it, a horrible mass uglier than anything in science-fiction, fattened by war, murder, starvation. Insatiable, waiting like a frog with a perennially pulsating neck, waiting to pick off fresh victims with a flick of its tongue. Someday, I'll start to count its victims from the past millennium. Maybe tomorrow.

Even if I were to erase from my mind the image of the bloated frog, ugly as it is, I can find nothing better. It's hard to believe the millennium is not yet over and that many unimaginable horrors are just waiting to surface. It scares the shit out of me until I remind myself that perhaps I might escape because I'm someone special. What a feast this has been. Surely the last thousand years belong to maggots. They crawl through my nightmares, until I am one of them, crawling with them through fields of flesh. As I stood beside Tetsuo, I was home in Field once again. I could almost see the sunlight bouncing off the peaks, dusted with fresh snow from the night before, and crashing into the river - where the river flowed free of its shell of ice - in a torrent of molten copper. This was, to me, my special dawn of creation. It didn't happen every morning, just once in a while, perhaps like the great Cambrian explosion that Mr. Kerrigan had so painstakingly explained to us in class one day. He had called it God's moment of creation. How beautiful it all seemed to me then.

I often think of the sunlight I could see from my room, the cradle of my childhood, just as often as I think of running through the woods which skirted our backyard. Often, as I ran, the newly risen sun, glowing almost white, flashed at me through the tall trees and branches like the intermittent beams from a lighthouse. The thick bed of pine needles strewn under the trees felt so soft that I had the sense of flying in space. It was as if my feet never felt the ground, never touched anything hard.

Sometimes, the same early morning sun bathed the canopy of spruce trees in a delicate orange, suggesting the approach of autumn. But autumn would be months away and wouldn't in any case force any changes to those trees. Why did I run? Why couldn't I stand among the trees, be one of them, free of the power that melds me to my body?

Thanks to Martin's parting words, I have often thought about the black hole too. Awake, I have stopped short of plunging into the great abyss on many occasions. Some days, it looked so warm, inviting, innocent like an evening sky blushing its welcome to the night's mysteries. Those were moments of the cruellest punishment for me. Those were days I had had enough of the ruins of my life, the barren, dusty stretches that separated me from other lives, lives I had wished to touch. The abyss cried out to me to rush into its fold, cool, verdant, downy. Perhaps I'd be one with the pre-Cambrian globs that were truly the beginnings of human life, and not Mr. Kerrigan's deception, the moment of God's creation.

Thanks to Augustine, however, nothing can wring out of my soul any more those piercing cries of despair I tried so hard to stifle into whispers to myself. Now, I am able to transform them into songs. But when the song is over, I'm never sure whether I have been mocking myself.

I had to tell someone about my encounter with Augustine. It turned out to be Tetsuo, looking tragic and bleary-eyed from the night before.

What a relief! Finally, I had finished reading *Confessions*. I remember shutting the book with a deep sigh and getting up from my chair, taking care to move slowly so the metal legs wouldn't rattle on the concrete floor. As I stretched myself and felt a warm glow surge through my back, my legs and arms, I was surprised how considerate I felt. Normally, I would have pushed the chair away from me happily creating the metallic din that was part of the nature of steel chairs. The pale light from my desk lamp bathed the faded green cover of the book with a wholeness and delicacy which matched the feelings suffusing my mind. "I was confounded and converted." Those words from the book kept echoing in my ears and made me feel rather good about myself.

For a while, Sam, who looked after the prison library, thought I was preparing for a full and complete disclosure of my crimes. I remember his eyes lighting up behind his thick lenses as he checked out the book for me.

"Confessions?" asked Sam. "Wonder how many years he served?"

"He wasn't a hood, you jerk," I corrected him. "He was a saint."

"Oh," Sam shrugged his shoulders, losing interest, his eyes reverting to their natural, half closed, state. "Tell me if you find it interesting."

Now that I think of it, I realize how hard some saints have tried to beat the rap and how often they failed. I felt somehow fulfilled I had finally finished St. Augustine's *Confessions*. Over the next few nights, I lay awake and thought I heard the footfalls of his God tearing through the walls of my cell, stopping next to my bed. But I didn't feel any closer to God, however one is able to judge this closeness. Rather, I felt I was nearing a total understanding of the puzzle that had obsessed me these last seven years. Perhaps the puzzle was my God. But how could I be certain?

Some prisoners have told me they have seen God walk softly through the winding corridors that seem coiled round our cells like a snake. I haven't seen God but I've seen the dark outlines of the guard tower poised like a snake's hood against the night sky, two yellow searchlights on either side of the hood fixed upon us like a snake's pitiless eyes. But I have also looked beyond the guard tower at the moon wrapped in a grey shawl of clouds blowing in the wind and I have felt a presence I cannot describe. Other prisoners have said God had seized their souls, filling them with remorse, purging their criminal minds of feelings of guilt and shame. I have been less fortunate.

✳ ✳ ✳

FOUR

During the night, I had discovered another piece of Marek's writing, lost in a stack of electricity bills and rent receipts. Tetsuo insisted that, when Connie returned in the morning, this would be our homage to Marek for that day. There were three songs, and we took turns reciting them.

ANGELS' SONG

"Ghetto Angel." I sang the song.

I am Marek Rubinstein, Yahweh's fool.
You wonder why I write, so do I.
By day, so cool, I'm so cool,
Through a rabbit's dusty warren
My eyes see neither light nor sky,
At night, chained to a roaring storm
Lashing fields of fire,
I wait for deliverance and cry.

Day after day I count my breath.
What cruel mockery, this life after death;
I've died, it seems so long ago,
Like Dathan and Abiram
Defying Moses and Aaron,
Condemned to *Sheol,*

183

My bones still moist, sinews crawling under
Pale skin banished from the sun,
My voice echoing in an endless swirl.

Doomed to every pain, every guilt on earth,
I die in life and play my death
On and on, for I have lost my God -
Oh God! pity this fool;
Accept his thanks to thee in Sheol?

O, let me find in Sheol my rest,
In whose darkness I'll tear my breast.
Rip out offerings to the pit
And pray, "You're a loving father."
I'll throw a kiss to the worm:
"To my mother, my sister,
And children unborn."

As I stormed along Chlodna one day
A crumpled piece of paper flew my way.
"We cannot promise you anything," it said,
"There's no assurance that all is well.
But certain the time has come
We'll bring you face to face a poet, now gone.
From his words draw courage.
So join us, we pray,
July eighteenth, four thirty p.m. Saturday.
Something more than words - atmosphere;
Emotion surpassed - turmoil;
These wasted actors, children all,
To life, applaud them back.
The admission is free -
Signed Goldszmit Korczak.

My youth spent studying the poet,
Dreaming of Santiniketan.
I had to see the play.
I crawled along Sliska Street,
Craving a seat at the table
Hiding like a rat
As I watched the fable.

They called the play *"Post Office"*,
The poet's name for it - *"Daak Ghawr"*.
Korczak never missed a point.
How correct, how proper.
The poet knew, I suspect Korczak too,
That "Daak Ghawr" is "the house that calls."
That's where we're headed,
The children, Korczak and I,
The whole wide world.
That night, as the curtain falls.

We were no strangers, Dr. Korczak and I.
Shamelessly I called to him
Taunting him in the street.
He in his Polish uniform
Worn and crumpled, hot in the sun,
Begging for potatoes in Stawki,
Wandering streets cobbled with hunger, fear,
Cajoling friends for money.
Or a drop of tear.

Loving foster parents in a stinking home
Cared for Amal, frail and alone,
Dreaming of hillsides lined with moss
The threshold a ring of fire

He dared not cross.
Two hundred Amals in Sliska Street,
Thousands more in the *Wohnbezirk*.
They lie where we laid them, me and my team,
Their molten flesh on fire,
Our tears hissing like steam.

"Angel of Life." Connie sang this song.

I have been a gardener all my life,
An endless store of seeds was mine to plant
In eager minds untouched by shame, ideas
I scattered in measured fists, free of strife,
Watered and nurtured to glorious life.

The winds of war through my garden roared,
Uprooting all, leaving a useless hoard,
Ideas that rot the mind, mutate,
Their withered roots crawl out my nose, my ears,
My eyes cracked and hardened in salted tears.

I an ungainly tree, around me lies
A desert where nothing stirs but sighs.
The desert struck terror in my heart.
I reached out for a word, a touch.
They slipped through my fingers like sand.
Naked I stood, no birds nested in me,
Amidst blood and fire and columns of smoke,
I watched the sun shrink to darkness and pain
And the moon bleed again and again.

I took pleasure in what little I had,
Laid dead friends in the ground like plants

Watered by fire, lulled by *kaddish*.
I passed Janusz Korczak on the road to heaven.
Strange, since I was he.

"Do you remember," he asked, "the great fire,
The one that burned the Torah scrolls?"
"Well, yes and no," I replied,
"For only the parchment burned, the letters flew
Up to heaven and were saved, were they not?"
"Yes they were," he said, "but God's anger,
Invincible, wouldn't spare the Jews;
He took a pen and wrote their sentence down -
Every Jew must be killed."
"Every Jew?" I asked, I laughed,
For we were in the millions, however damned,
Fearful we had lost the promised land.

"Yes, every last Jew is doomed,
Not a soul to be spared.
But the letters flew in fright,
Hid in the clouds, dissolved God's purpose
So he could not write."

Remember, Germans are men, not God,
Their furnaces bricks and steel,
One day they'll burn but leaves
And crumble soon to dust
While our Spirit breathes.

The doctor waved a weary hand
And crossed the gates to heaven.
Alone in a million, six million, stood I.

Where shall I run, where hide,
O Death! my eternal bride?

Spun in the web of mothers' wombs,
I am *nephesh*, the gossamer breath of life.
Embroidered in sleep in a forest of dreams
By a poet now dust.
His words poured like milk,
A softly curdling cheese, defying every blight,
Behind the mist of an embrace
And a kiss each night.

Abrasha I am, for a moment brief
As evening shadows cast a pall,
With lights and paint on the stage of life,
Under the poet's spell, I'm Amal.

I wait for Sudha through eternity,
She promised me flowers.
I'll wait, counting the days, the hours.

"Angel of Death." Ironically, this would have to be Tetsuo's
song.

Before I die let me sing of death;
Lift my eyes to the sea, a sea of peace.
Help me sail the sea,
Deaf to voices that bid me stay.
Hurry me to the space between sun and moon
By stardust blown
Face to face with the great Unknown.

I had a noble friend, he said,
"What songs, when all about are dying?

Thousands must be fed."
He would have me burn my brush
With which I paint my birds
Soaring in the sky.

"The birds have had their food, their rest;
New blood drives their wings on high.
Hunger stalks the land.
What use the shedding of a tear?
I cannot sing songs from Kabir.
Let Tagore spin like others,
Burn his foreign clothes."
So said my friend,
While I listened.

Others said I was a Jew, my name Rabbi Nathan,
My wife an Oppenheimer,
A bamboo dealer's daughter in Bombay.
So I am, so I'm not.
I'm Amal too and more -
Sailor, farmer, whore.
Now my voice is frail;
Are my songs to no avail?

We are to the gods as insects are to us.
They perish by the million,
We go our way;
We die in thousands and still we pray.
But on the field of Kurukshetra
Krishna did say:
"I've been born many times, Arjun,
And many times have you.

But I remember past lives;
Ah! forgetful you."

What an infinite blessing, what a cruel jest.
That I was born to sing,
For a single life my spirit longs.
O! let me remember words, the songs.

* * *

Voice Four: Marek

Four-One

I have done my duty. I think that's the last of Marek's papers that I will read in his apartment. But I'll continue to read him. Not because I think it'll form a good habit, but because Marek Rubenstein was a good man. The nearness of him might someday make me a better person. I'm glad I was able to do it the last four days. The rest of the day gets so choked up with the business of living - grocery shopping, cashing cheques, paying bills, visiting, answering phone messages. It'll be different in prison, I know. Some day, I'll be free. By evening, we should be out of here. Where do I go from here? Oh! I've not forgotten.

Marek's song keeps echoing in my mind. I thought of Stan as I heard Tetsuo read those last lines, and I thought of Martin Fisher, my father. Of course, there's another reason to be thinking of Martin. He's coming back to Warsaw. Connie came back from a quick trip to her apartment to say there was a message on her answering machine. He'll not be here this evening too. What Connie didn't tell me at the time was that Martin Fisher had boarded a flight to Frankfurt, rented a car, set out towards Koblenz along the Rhine Valley. He had stopped for the night at the clifftop hotel in Loreley. The next morning, there were no signs of the man. His car was still in the parking lot and all his things in his room. Martin Fisher had simply vanished.

Many months later, after an unusually short visit by Mr. Nowakowski, the lawyer, I was to discover the clue to Martin Fisher's secret passion that might have led him to the Loreley Hotel that October evening. This was no Burgess Ridge, but once upon a time, it must have been a wild, tumultuous site throbbing with the bloodlust of the likes of Hagen and Krimhilde. I could see in the final mysterious disappearance of my father a repudiation of all the order and the civility that had been hammered into him. Sure, hard work pays off. For certain, patience brings home some results. But the lost treasure of Hagen is still worth the plunge from the heights of Loreley. For this one single act, this triumphant glob of spit in the face of propriety, I was able to forgive my father for all the wrongs he had inflicted on us in the name of rationality.

Mr. Nowakowsky left behind a parcel. He said it contained some personal items the police had found among Martin Fisher's personal belongings left behind in the German clifftop hotel. One part of my mind couldn't wait to open the package. Another part prodded me towards patience and indifference. Just then, I felt a terrible itch on my arm where the faint shadows of the mysterious pigmentation still attracted my attention from time to time. I let my fingers wander over the spot, lovingly caressing the skin. The mark had all but disappeared. I made up my mind to open the package. Quickly and impatiently I ripped off the paper covering. Inside, in a transparent plastic bag was something that looked very much like an old shawl or a scarf. I had never seen it before in my father's possessions. As I carefully slipped the folded material out of the bag, its feel and its somewhat musty smell reminded me right away of something similar I had seen on Marek - a *tallit*, Marek's prayer shawl. What could Martin Fisher be doing with a *tallit*, I wondered?

The folded shawl felt heavier than it looked. I soon discovered there were some other objects wrapped in its folds. As I opened the folds, there rolled out before my eyes two incredible pieces of *tefillen* and a *yarmulke*. I had never seen them on Martin, but I knew that they were from Marek. My fingers began to shake as I picked up the *tefillen shel yad* and the *tefillen shel rosh*. But the fingers steadied soon and, with a stubborn determination, I tied the leather straps of the *tefillen* - one around my forehead, the other around my hand. A sudden peace spread through my body and tears streamed down my cheeks. But my lips remained sealed. The prayers I never learnt lay locked in my heart.

I remembered Loreley, and one day I went to see her. There she was, sitting demurely on the clifftop, her back to the dappled pastures laden with mist and cattle, have you not seen Martin Fisher? Fischer spelt with a thoughtfully discarded 'c.' Loreley, Loreley, was it your song that drew him to you? Was it your refrain rippling in the waters below that lured him onto the rocks?

How dramatic. The muted greens, yellows, and exploding crimson of the fall in the background. Preposterous castles poking through the forests like monster limbs erupting from the earth. The ruins of the Gothic chapel of St. Werner at Bacharach staring through hollow naves like a giant skull mounted on the hillside. The muddy waters of the Rhine curving in froth across the steel bows of barges - some with a solitary red cross on their flag, others with strips of red, white and blue, or yellow, red and black - with such names as *Veronica, Starlight, Albatross,* and *Magdalena*. Contented burghers walking their shimmering dogs along the banks. Trains sliding along both sides of the river with incessant regularity. The vines on the slopes regenerating themselves from generation to generation. Furtive Turks pushing babies in creaking prams. Gulls and ducks swirling over the water, breaking their flight awkwardly to spear an occasional prey. And all this within sight of the Hercynian massifs, not to mention Archbishop Hatto's Mouse Tower. He couldn't have planned it better. Martin, the unswerving believer in systems, did he really repudiate all in the end?

Talk of the haunting memory of the Burgess Shale. I have no doubt that billions of years from now, some intelligent form of life will discover, beautifully preserved in shale, the body of Martin Fisher. And the discovery will generate the same sense of excitement as the discovery of *Pikaia*, or *Marrella*, or *Alalcomenaeus*. And perhaps the same sense of wonder about where the creatures all vanished from the face of the earth.

Or it could be that as he stood on one of the spurs below Loreley and contemplated the Rhine, a hand reached out from the clouds above and plucked him physically off the face of the earth. Such things have been known to happen before.

Connie has made up her mind to return to L.A. Just like that. I should have known. I think I've been kidding myself all along that there was some kind of a future for us together. But when you're nineteen, the future gapes at you like a cosmic hole, you're certain you can make the fateful leap that'll make the hole - call it an abyss if you will - no more frightening than a puddle of water in the street. However gilded and seductive its edges, the outer rim, if you look inside deep enough, and hard enough, all you can see is the astronomer's black hole. You can't see the future for the blackness. What a rave it was the other day when we made love by the book. I wonder if there was anything in the book to hold us together. If there was, surely Connie would've told me. "Dearest Matthew," she said to me last night, "many of us never learn that there's more to life than getting ahead, moving up, fucking, and getting progressively fucked up. Sometimes you have to wait a long time until the streetcar you want comes along."

"Sometimes, the streetcar may never show up," I suggested gloomily. As one gets older, I suppose one becomes more full of doubt.

"That's been known to happen," she said in response, "although I am certain Tetsuo would have an answer for your dilemma. He's absolutely wonderful with dilemmas."

Nineteen is such a curious age, I thought. The gene machine is primed and ready to go. It's an age when one is a human entity, but hardly a human character. So I wouldn't be surprised if Tetsuo saw no substance in my dilemma - whether to wait for the streetcar of my choice or jump onto the first one that came rattling my way and caught my fancy. At nineteen, my dilemmas, if any, were so immediate, so unlike Hamlet's earth-shattering ones. If I were Hamlet, some of my lines might be "To dream or not to dream," "To snort or not to snort," or even "To fuck Cordelia or let her die a stupid, ignorant virgin." But these lines are so common, so everyday, that I can't imagine Shakespeare, who wrote with an eye for kings and queens and lords, ever including them in his plays. Slick Willy, that poet, even though the peasants loved him too.

Prison gave me my voice. I have come round to believing that sixteen is a good age to go to prison.

Why does Connie seem withdrawn? She came early enough, but then said she had to return to the apartment to pick up a few things. She came back to give me my father's message, and promised to see me at lunchtime. There's no work for her to go to, so I assume she has some errands to run, especially if she was thinking of leaving the city soon. At the time, I wondered if my father had had a change of heart. If so, what did it portend?

My deliverance wasn't going to be easy. I had to find my own way to the hole, the swamp, the post-office. I decided it was all one and the same. I would stumble into it in my own time. Did I have my own place beside my mother in the black hole? Did I not love her once, like my father? I told Connie I would rather be with her, that I didn't want to be emotionally blackmailed by Martin Fisher if he should show up again. Once one of the Fuehrer's loyal soldiers. Then an upright Canadian citizen. Brave fire fighter from the Gulf War. Who knows how many other lives he has up his sleeve. Connie merely smiled and said, "Just don't blackmail yourself."

Was Connie teasing me? Was she suggesting that I was blackmailing myself into staying back with her? Tetsuo, the destroyer of dilemmas, was coming with his car for our final ride from Marek's home. This was to be our irrevocable farewell to Marek, and none of us would want to miss the collective experience for anything in the world. There were so many other farewells of late. Connie and I sat facing each other across the dinner table, the space separating us wide and seemingly unbridgeable. It was all emptiness and silence. Marek would have wished it this way.

"Never regret what happened between us. It was real, if only for a moment in time. I know it was, it is, real because we caused no one any pain. Not to Lydia, not to Tetsuo."

"Not to Lydia, not to Tetsuo," I repeated after her. "But what about ourselves? Does that mean nothing?"

"Of course it does," she said. But it's our own, to keep, to remember. No one takes it away from us.

"You've been with Tetsuo too long," I said. Connie turned to me and kissed me lightly on my lips. "Are you going to go back to him?" I asked.

"He hasn't invited me back yet. Our relationship hasn't been the same since I lost the baby. Tetsuo's still warm and caring, but he's also more remote from the urgent needs and nagging preoccupations of others."

"But you're waiting for a letter, aren't you?" I asked. "Sort of like Amal."

"Amal didn't get his letter, did he?"

"Depends on what you mean by a letter," I replied after thinking about it for a moment. "That's probably why Marek never reconciled himself to the ending." I walked over to Connie and held her by the shoulders and felt her fragrance rise to my face. "Tell me just once," I asked. "Tell me how it happened to him."

She knew what I wanted to know. "We let the water drain out of the tub," she said. "It was fascinating to watch the red getting lighter and lighter as the level of water fell in the tub. Finally, the gurgling at the drain and the clanking sounds from the decrepit plumbing stopped. Patches of red from larger clots of blood clung to the sides of the white tub. But Marek looked pale and even whiter, his eyes staring motionless at something, it would seem, that lay beyond time and space. We hauled Marek out of the tub and laid out the body on the floor. Puddles of water formed on the fading linoleum floor as the last drops of water rolled off the body.

"It was then that I noticed Marek's arm. I was astounded to see he had the same skin pigmentation that you had been suffering from - a swath of whiteness going round the arm with a bluish tinge, much like what one sees in a bruise, spread on the skin like a Star of David.

A disquieting discovery, and it filled me with a sense of mystery and wonder. I wish I had something like it myself. There would've been something to show for the kinship that had grown between Marek and me. "Now I have nothing," I said simply.

I racked my brain trying to understand why Marek had grown the patch on his arm. Of course, the obvious answer seemed to be that he was Jewish. I wasn't. So, why did I develop the condition in the first place? If one were to say that the Star of David on my arm became a symbol of emotional solidarity with Marek, why did I want it to fade away? Did I feel any differently towards him before it happened to me? If, genetically speaking, the infection was indeed a form of mimicry, could it be the case of a parasite, whose genes aspire to the same destiny as the genes of its host, eventually sharing all the interests of its host and ceasing to act parasitically. What if I had become, in a manner of speaking, a Jew? In a sense, what could be a stronger proof of my love for Marek and Olga. Now I no longer needed to carry any cards, any tokens, signs or symbols. Our oneness came straight from the heart, went straight to the heart. Matthew no longer needed to pretend to be different from Misha, Misha no longer needed to masquerade to win Lydia's love. I was whole again. The infection, if one may call it that, had made us one.

Four-Two

At that moment, thanks to Connie's revelation, I imagined I was looking once again into Marek's eyes. All the stories he had told me - during our walks, over cups of coffee - all came flooding into my mind. I didn't find him gazing into space, as dead people often do, into nothingness. I was amazed how beautiful death can make a person sometimes. In fact, I found him staring right into my soul. And there, in a flash, I saw what he had seen, found the knowledge he had not shared with me in life. In Marek's eyes I discovered the reflection of my soul and the secret of my beginnings. This was the swamp he had been a witness to. A swamp infested with tongues of fire curling through a lace of steel on which slept Julek and Giena, Eva and Halinka, Jakub and Leon, Mietek and Abus, Hanna and Adzio, Zygmus, Sami, Hanka, Aronek, Hella, Mendelek, Adek, Jerzyk, Chaimek, even Abrasha. There were all the others from Krochmalna Street, from Chlodna Street, from Sienna Street and Sliska Street, hundreds of them, countless thousands. Marek laid them tenderly on the grates, each one of them - Stefa, Korczak, little Romcia - muttering a verse I had so often heard him mutter to himself:

> For a day of vengeance was in my heart,
> And my year of redemption had come.
> I looked, but there was none to help,
> I looked in amazement, but there was
> none to uphold;
> So my own arm helped me
> And my fury upheld me.
>
> *[Trito-Isaiah lxiii.4,5]*

199

The tongues of fire engulfed them all, lovingly like lotus petals, and drew them into the raging lake.

I realized a change had come over me when I found that my sense of smell wasn't troubling me any more. Now I could smell nothing, neither the fragrant flowers nor the burning flesh. I had lost my sense of smell. At other times, such a loss might have devastated me for it normally worked like a compass for me, steering me away from objects of revulsion towards objects of desire. But I had no regrets. In fact, there rose a fleeting question in my mind as to what might happen if every other sense abandoned my body one by one. If I had a choice, I wonder what I would part with last of all.

No time to speculate, for I was in Marek's swamp, his beloved garden, his house that calls forever, each echo a farewell to generations past, a welcome to generations new. It seemed I entered this world through Marek's open eyes from which there stretched a laser-like path leading to my innermost being. A fierce blizzard raged around me, the roar of thunder rose from my throbbing heart. Through the blinding storm a piece of crumpled paper flew into my face. What was it? A letter perhaps, the precious letter from the King that Amal had been waiting for? I plucked it eagerly off my face and read:

> *We cannot promise you anything for we have no assurance that all is well. But we are certain the time has come to bring you close to the words of a certain poet and philosopher, words which will move you to strong feelings. For this reason we invite you to come and join us on Saturday, the 18th of July, at 4:30 o'clock in the afternoon.*

You will find inscribed, on this invitation, the
verses of Wladyslaw Szlengel, ghetto poet:

> *Something more than words*
> *The atmosphere ...*
> *Something more than emotion ·*
> *The turmoil ...*
> *Something more than actors*
> *The children ...*

Free admission

Signed: *Dr. Goldszmit Korczak*
Orphanage Director

Free admission. Amazing. I ate the invitation. It was the
last thing I had on me. The Doll just looked at me and smiled.
He pointed with his thumb to the left, then cracked his whip
on his boot as I moved forward.

Suddenly, I was Abrasha, one of the Doctor's orphans.

Of course, I've never seen the doctor. I haven't seen him
from the time we boarded the train. He would've hated the
boxcar, such a stickler for cleanliness. All day long we wal-
lowed in shit, people peed where they lay, moaned for water,
took off their clothes in the heat, then licked the sweat off
each other's bodies. Early this morning - I knew it was morning because I hadn't blacked out yet and the sky was purple
like the dead faces in the wagon - how their eyes stare back
like clouded glass, their twisted lips parted around the tips
of their tongue wait for the feel of water. Too late. Early this
morning somebody passed me a bowl with a little water.
Before my lips could touch it, a woman tried to snatch the

bowl away. "My son needs it," she said. I decided to ignore her, and lifted the bowl to my mouth. Before I could drink a drop she sank her teeth into my wrist. I gave her the cup. My blood tasted heavenly, warm; it almost tasted like bread. The doctor would tell us how his great grand-father was a glazier, how glass gave him warmth and light. Not those glass eyes, neither surprised, nor fearful, in death.

I think I've told you I'm Abrasha. I'm seventeen. It's easy to forget when things happen so fast, when thoughts crowd the mind and rush forward as we seem to be doing. It's go-go-go from the moment we tumbled out of the wagons. The large station clock said three. When I looked at it after what seemed an age, just as we were being herded out of the station, the clock still said three. Which was rather odd. The clock looked pretty, as pretty as the signs which read *Station Obermajdan....Change here for Bialystok and Wolkowysk.* Other signs hanging from a high wire carried instructions for bathing and disinfection. And the clock still said three. As we were leaving the platform I knew the clock was merely a picture, newly painted just like everything else - the door leading to the waiting room, the ticket windows. Wonder of wonders, there was even a Post Office with a postal wicket, a red mailbox even. But there was no postman inside, no postal lady or clerk. But that didn't strike me as odd, for it could be that I was destined to be the new postman.

I think most of us knew where we were coming to. The Doctor had called me aside and told me before we left Sliska Street. Yes, I guess I had seen him after all. We had started walking in the heat of noon, now we're walking again. *Judenscheisse*, jewish shit, they called us in Warsaw. And the doctor would tell me: "Those who lack a nation, must roam the seas; yes, some will drown in the waves; all will drown in the waves." Doctor Korczak looked out of the windows of his solitary study on Krochmalna Street, his eyes misty, his shoulders slumped with fatigue. I was afraid then, I was afraid when we set out to board the boxcars at the *Umschlagplatz*, I'm not afraid anymore.

For I have played out my death once before. It seems like yesterday that half of Warsaw answered the Doctor's invitation and came to see us do *The Post Office*. But I know it wasn't yesterday. "Why *The Post Office*?" I asked him. "Because one must accept the angel of death," he replied. Doesn't matter any more whether it was yesterday when I stood behind the curtains, waiting nervously, impatiently, for my turn. Chaimek, the doctor was funny, even though he wasn't meant to be.

Dead serious, he said, "On no account must Amal be let out of doors," and I, Amal, could barely keep myself from laughing.

Madhav protested, "It's so hard, so difficult to keep him inside all day long."

"It's got to be done," insisted the doctor. "Fall brings sickness. The sunshine and the wet winds are both equally dangerous, harmful. For it's written in the holy books ....." And he would launch into one of his frequent homilies.

But look, the storm, the lightning, the rain, nothing harms me any more. Yes, I was Amal, the sick child. Forbidden to step outdoors, I could only stand at the edge of the courtyard and recite my opening lines. I begged to be let out to where my aunt ground the lentils in the quirn, where the squirrel sat with his tail up in the air and stuffed the broken grains in his mouth. "Can't I run up there, uncle?" I asked of Madhav.

I wished I were a squirrel. I longed to go beyond the hills I could see from my window.

"Now listen," said Madhav, "since that hill stands there solid as a wall, it means you can't get beyond it. Else, what was the point of heaping together so many large stones to make such a big affair!"

"Uncle," I asked, "do you think it's meant to prevent you from crossing over? It seems to me because the earth can't speak it raises its hands to the sky and beckons. Those who live far away and sit alone by their windows can read the message."

We were shuffling past the engine standing in front of the train that had brought us here, brought us east for resettlement as they told us. As we walked past the same engine in Warsaw I overheard the doctor turn to Miss Stefa and say, "If only yesterday's actors could continue in their roles today." I have often thought about this. Except that it wouldn't have helped me much since I was expected to die at the end of "The Post Office" anyway. And yet, I didn't die, for I came out, holding hands with Devorah and Jerzyk, to bow as the audience applauded. Didn't I?

This place looks so fresh and clean and proper. I'm sure there are some among us who will fool themselves till the very end. But for something in the air, a whiff of something strange and repulsive, this place smells fresh and new. Everything was clean and orderly at the station until a young girl started to cry. "I'm young, I want to work," she wailed, as she darted towards the column on the right. Two soldiers leapt in her direction and dragged her away from the crowd until she was alone, cowering in the sunlight. Suddenly, a smiling man in military uniform appeared on a white horse as if from nowhere. "The Baron," rose a whisper from the guards. In an instant, the horse was upon the woman, kicking and trampling her beneath its hooves. She screamed once, then fell silent as her lifeless, bloodied body wilted beside a bed of flowers.

I looked around as someone clutched my hand. Jerzyk was there beside me, a frightened look in his eyes. He looked hunched, his knees bent, as if he was trying to grow smaller than he was. I also saw Devorah immediately behind me and stopped. Our bodies touched and I put my arms around her. After all, she was Sudha, the flower girl, in "The Post Office", and I had always loved her secretly. Jerzyk was the fakir who visited me in my sickness. He came from the Isle of Parrots, that land of wonders, that haunt of birds, where they simply sing and fly among the green hills, and flock back on their green wings with the red glow of the sunset on the hillside. What great lines they had in the play, both Devorah and Jerzyk. Devorah looked pale and sick; sicker than I. I stared at her eyes until the sharp crack of a whip across my face brought me home to the reality of stinging pain and blood spurting out of my nose.

We quickened our pace. The sound of whips whistling in the air became more and more frequent. We were afraid to talk, even children were afraid to cry. As I turned my face instinctively to catch the eyes of my assailant, I also saw work crews hauling out the dead from the wagons. I wondered whether they were Jews like me, but it really didn't matter. As the columns from the left and right marched forward towards the barbed wire fence in the distance, The Doll leapt into a car and was soon lost amid the barracks and watchtowers up ahead.

The crowd walked through a large gate behind which stood a cluster of buildings looking much like barracks. I was weary. I was thirsty. The sight of the barracks offered a passing hope that we might eventually lie down on bunks or even on the floor. The sound of music which had greeted our ears even as we left the station now filled the air with a fresh burst of energy. I saw an orchestra under a tree not far away, four musicians with yellow patches on their shirts working away at a flute, a double bass, and a couple of violins. I didn't know their music. Summer had covered with thick leaves a grove of trees which lined the west side of the camp where the sun was beginning to go down. I could have given in to a sense of peace which the trees, the neat buildings, the music and the warm sunset sky suggested, had it not been for the Spanish horses covered with barbed wire and fresh branches marking the camp perimeter. And the guards, they were chasing us now. "Faster, faster," hissed the guards. That's when I once again saw The Doll, whose name was like a wave of electricity that shot through the crowd the moment we clambered out of the railcars.

I was standing face to face with The Doll as he pointed to the left or right. The next moment I was alone even as I stood in a line of hundreds. We had passed The Doll. Devorah was gone, chased into the barracks on the left with other women and children. Jerzyk had fallen behind, and I never saw him again. Perhaps he will tend to his waterfall on Parrot's Isle where the water tumbles down like molten diamonds and makes the pebbles sing as the water rushes over them to the sea. Maybe the Fakir would come to terms with the birds and build himself a small cabin among their crowd of nests and pass eternity counting the sea waves.

The music died down as we ran into a narrow passage with a sign which read *Himmelstrasse*, The Road to Heaven. There was even a curtain which must have seen better days in some synagogue. We had to lift this curtain as we ran into the Road to Heaven. Guards with truncheons and dogs on easy leashes lined the passage. The truncheons came down on us, the dogs mauled us along the way. A short while later, the passage was joined by another passage through which came running a stream of women, some cradling children in their arms. Shorn of their hair, they looked more naked than men. I suppose Devorah might've been among them, but there was no way to tell. Devorah, Sudha. Sudha, Devorah. Sudha, the flower-seller's daughter who walked by my window on her way to gathering flowers, with her feet so light and the anklets jingling happily as she walked. "Be good and sit still," she said, "and on my way back home I'll bring you some flowers."

So here I am, waiting to bathe with hundreds of other bodies, some broken, some already dead! We screamed in pain every time a whip or a truncheon cut into our flesh. At one point one of the guards stood brandishing a sabre, which he brought down, to the accompaniment of hideous screams, across women's breasts, as we were driven along the Road to Heaven. Otherwise, everyone was deathly quiet; if one listened, all one heard was the sound of panting. I can't even hear that now anymore. In this room, it's as if we have all stopped breathing. To think that Devorah might be in the same room as me. Ah! lips that will be unkissable in a matter of time, breasts that will turn into dust in time. Time. And it'll still be three o'clock on the station clock at Treblinka.

I'm scared. Not of death, but of dying. I would've gladly walked to my death holding the doctor's hand. He was a father to me, as he had been to hundreds before me. There's so much to tell. The wonderful concerts in Krochmalna Street. Walking hand in hand with Miss Stefa along the Vistula. Is this place more real than the river? The room's not too large. It looks like a regular shower room with everything one would find in a public bathhouse. The walls are covered with small white tiles, pretty fine work. I saw the floor covered with orange terra cotta tiles. We are so jammed against one another now that I can't see the floor. Nickel-plated metal faucets stare down at us from the ceiling. I haven't caught my neighbours' eyes yet, for everyone it seems is looking up at the faucets.

A strange silence has come down upon us. We are afraid to breathe lest we break the spell. "Ivan, water!" screamed a shrill voice outside the doors.

At first there was a hissing sound, then an overpowering smell, then a babble of voices. Some cried, "Sh'ma Yisroel!" A small voice whimpered, "Oy vey, Mama!" Then came the screams, and the flailing arms, and the thrashing. We were moving in an ocean, gaining ground towards some distant shore every moment.

Suddenly, a piece of the now familiar music crashes through the locked doors with the fury and violence of an explosion. Gradually, it fades into a whisper. Every other sound is now stilled. The ocean swirls around the shore, licking the over-hanging rocks once in a while, but mostly it is content to leave behind swishing arches of foam on the sand. While this was taking place, one forgot that the wind was busy, gathering its strength in silence. One never knew when it happened, but suddenly the wind had unleashed its invisible force, prodding the waves to a drunken madness, until the waves came crash-ing behind the music like souls driven with whips of remorse, without a pause, without a sigh, and the foam vanished the instant the waves crashed on the sand. Equally indistinct was the moment the wind died down and the sea returned to its casual, almost bored, playfulness.

As the violins died down, some seamless voice rose in a triumphant prayer, keeping pace with the cello's sombre remonstrance. The voice rose with every mounting note from the organ until it touched the clouds and disappeared; the strings poked around down in the orchestra pit like the playful ocean etching foam images on the sand.

Later, the harp mingles with the voice in a recurring wail, rising slowly like the mist, only to fall back under its weight until the voice breaks free like a comet hurtling through space. Crystalline, the voice is like a shriek trapped in melody, a gentle embrace that wraps pain and despair within its arms.

The sea thickens. It's not water any more, it's blood. Her voice would drown in the pool of blood if only she would let it, if only she refused to fight. But not she, she who refused even to look at the chains that held her to the ground. The sea is a pool of tears and blood that'll never dry out, the wind a chorus of sighs unwilling to be silenced. Sighs ripped out of human hearts trampled on the ground, ground to dust. The last sighs of broken spirits that must surely win the reprieve of defiance some day.

It was time to go, My days of reprieve were over. The remaining days of my sentence hung before me like a tapestry, as dark and forbidding as those on courtly palace walls. They covered not marble, but prison walls and iron bars. And then I realized they could well be a tapestry of ideas woven in solitude. Of course, the tapestry would be just that. A tapestry, not a revelation. But I had to believe in it.

The anxiety driving Matthew's pursuit of genetic knowledge, Misha's devotion to the love of others, both came face to face in the song. Suddenly, there was nothing separating the two. The song no longer echoed through my mind, and I thought it was unlikely to ever again in the future. But I longed to hear it again.

"We can listen to it whenever you want," promised Tetsuo. I found that very reassuring, almost exhilarating, because it meant Olga and Marek and I would still be holding hands at dusk while the music played. Lydia and I would still be in each others' arms while the music played. And if Connie were to bear my children someday, they too would inherit the music. And would they inherit the mark that seems burnt into my skin? Maybe, just maybe. I hope there's no shame in it for them. I hope.

And then I looked once more at my arm and noticed that the skin was totally free of any marks, the blemish that was once my shame and had lately, in its fading moments, begun to fill me with a sense of pride. There was now a feeling of relief, but also a sense of loss. And then the music started in my ears one more time. This time, I heard Martin Fisher reciting his prayers - something I had never heard him do before. My heart longed to join him in his prayers, but my lips wouldn't open. But as the music slowly died down I thought I could clearly hear the last words he said: "For the Lord your God is an impassioned God - lest the anger of the Lord your God blaze forth against you and He wipe you off the face of the earth."

And when the music lay stilled and Martin Fisher's voice faded away, I remembered. And I prayed.

- END -

On August 5, 1942, Dr. Korczak and two hundred children and inmates of the orphanage boarded railcars and went to their death in the gas chambers at Treblinka.